SIMPLY SEPARATE PEOPLE

Lynn Crawford

SIMPLY SEPARATE PEOPLE

[BLACK SQUARE EDITIONS]
[HAMMER BOOKS] [NEW YORK]

Copyright © 2002 by Lynn Crawford

ISBN 0-9712485-0-8

Published in the United States by
Black Square Editions
an imprint of Hammer Books
130 West 24th Street, #5A
New York, NY 10011

U.K. OFFICES

Four Walls Eight Windows/Turnaround
Unit 3, Olympia Trading Estate
Coburg Road, Wood Green
London N22 6TZ, England

FIRST PRINTING MARCH 2002

*Library of Congress
Cataloging-in-Publication
information on file*

Designed by Quemadura

All rights reserved. No part of this book may
be reproduced, stored in a data base or other
retrieval system, or transmitted in any form,
by any means, including mechanical, electronic,
photocopying, recording, or otherwise, without
the prior written permission of the publisher.

One's self I sing, a simple, separate person . . .

[WALT WHITMAN]

Banality in the landscape means the viewer.

[CARLA HARRYMAN]

For my father

RICHARD CRAWFORD

and mother

SOPHIE MCGEE

*I must thank these friends/family members
for certain support and inspiration:*

DASHURI ALIKO

JOHN CORBIN

AMY

ANNIE

BILL AND PENNY CRAWFORD

GINA FERRARI

CARLA HARRYMAN

PAUL KOTULA

PATRICK MCGEE

HARRY MATHEWS

VALERIE PARKS

IRMA RESTAINO

LYNNE TILLMAN

CHRIS TYSH

JENNIFER WERNER

PETER WILLIAMS

JOHN YAU

and my husband, Super Dad

JOHN HADDAD

CONTENTS

Physh
[1]

Pumper
[23]

Seamstress
[40]

Physh
[58]

Pumper
[99]

Seamstress
[127]

Bry
[142]

Physh
[178]

SIMPLY SEPARATE PEOPLE

PHYSH

I'm talking to DR, replaying events from memory. Yesterday he came here with tapes, lotion, and sparkling water; today he brings flowers and juice. *Here* is my studio apartment: bed, full bath, kitchen; linoleum, stereo, movie posters tacked onto wallpaper patterned with flowers, animals and vegetables.

DR, who once worked as an undercover agent, has seen scared people run to the upper flights of their home; I move to the top space in my building, I don't think out of fear. The rent is higher than my ground floor studio, but the space is larger, has more windows and a spectacular view. Do scared people quit school? I did; increased my hours at the music store, a change that helped financially. But otherwise, things seemed to unravel, like the needlework on my ottoman; the one DR gave me, embroidered by his sister.

SIMPLY SEPARATE PEOPLE

Last year his sister moved to town. Today he recommends me as her house and dog sitter, jobs she needs filled during the weeks and months she's off on global business. I haven't met DR's sister, though I have seen a picture of her dressed in a round bosomed top and knit skirt whose front slit exposes large knees. She's standing in a garden, or somewhere with ground cover, so you can't see her ankles or shoes.

Our first meeting is my interview. I enter her building lobby, a few blocks from mine. She—sweat shirt and pants, exercise sandals showing polished toes, rough heels—hands a bunch of chrysanthemums to the door person. His eyes fill with tears, she wipes them. I stand just inside the door breathing quietly, hear her say, Sorry for your loss, while re-drying his dripping eyes. She starts for his nose, also dripping, but he takes the cloth and dries it. I introduce myself; he sniffs; she takes my large, chapped hand in her large, well moisturized one, and leads me to a specially labeled elevator that shoots up and opens to her top floor apartment. A butcher-block table, holding a plate of powdered cookies, stands in her front hall. She takes two, hands me one, says, Come inside.

The apartment, like mine, sits at the edge of a huge, dirty city with narrow streets, unsanitary rivers, and earsplitting traffic. Unlike mine it is a gigantic co-op, and held together with a decoration theme: country. Complex flower, ivy and other plant arrangements; weave rugs, gingham-checked cushions. Different sized iron skillets line one kitchen wall; two antique distressed cabinets holding white plates, cups and pitchers line another. Her dog is enormous, thick coated.

Now for my observatory, she, lips white from the powdered cookie, says.

While what I saw downstairs was busy, rustic, up here is all space. Except for her metal urns, jars and the foliage that sometimes brims from them. And her telescopes. We examine her urns, jars, and telescopes. Without telescopes you can't separate figures individually, she explains, introducing my lesson on how to operate them. After the lesson, we lean over the balcony railings, scan the street. She points out a grocery, the river, a mailbox, when someone, carrying a ream of red fabric, enters the directly-across-the-street building. That, says DR's sister, is the Seamstress. A moment later a group of men and women carrying baskets enter the same building. They, says DR's sister, are her employees.

We walk down the winding stairs, through her living room, to her bed area. It's partitioned off by a dark brown divider, bordered with sunflowers and butter churns.

A row of multi-branched coat racks stands next to the screen (on the bedside area). Towels drape one rack, nightgowns another, jogging bras and shorts a third, aprons a fourth, blue jean overalls, soiled at the knees as if they'd been used for gardening, hangs by itself on the fifth.

Several feet in front of these racks, a slatted wood sleigh bed. Pillows embroidered with farm animals (a chicken, a cow, a pig) lie on its white spread.

In front of this bed, next to the window (the entire wall is a window; DR's sister explains to me the special glass lets us see out, but no one see in), a ski track exercise machine, and sets of free weights. She says I am free to use her equipment, though she understands her brother and I train regularly together at the gym.

She turns back to the bed, asks, Would I mind sleeping here? I say, No. She asks, would I mind sleeping with the dog on the bed with me? I say, No. She runs through other jobs she'd expect of me: cleaning, gardening (she has considerable balcony foliage, and co-op grounds duties), mail and message collection, dog walking; dog walking being the most important. She shows me the two leashes: one leather, one invisible. The invisible leash has two cuffs that are visible: one wraps around the walker's wrist, one around the animal's neck. (It has a switch; when on it engages a force that prevents the dog from straying). We use this device to take her dog to the park. I learn the specific routes (morning, lunch, evening); we shake hands, walk to our homes. Walking to my home, thinking of childhood—our big porch, big neighbors and green lawn—I pass a bakery whose windows are filled with trays of powdered cookies. I buy six, freeze three, save the rest for morning.

Next morning I sit down to them, the telephone rings; it is DR's sister, offering me a job as her house and dog sitter starting in six weeks.

During those weeks, I keep to my pattern: work, socialize, sleep. Wake; meet DR for our pre-work gym work-out. Repair my—just slightly—unraveling ottoman.

PHYSH

Six weeks crawl by, I leave the music store, my new job starts. The first morning, I stand on my employer's balcony, review my telescope lessons.

There's no wind; leaves which have fallen from trees litter the balcony terrace. I sweep and bag them. My eyes water, not from distress, but fall cold.

The afternoon stays dry. If it were windy, I'd fly my kite in the park. Instead, I stay up on the balcony, soon see the Seamstress, hair draping her shoulders, standing on a curb, yelling, TAXI!

I walk the dog, make a to do list, tape it to the refrigerator, take DR's sister's sports utility vehicle (parked in a lot around the corner) for a drive.

By the time I leave the city, reach bleating sheep, wheat and cornfields, churches with bells, I'm hours from home and my gas tank is on empty. So look for and find a fuel station. I beep; a woman appears, introduces herself as the Pumper, takes my order, answers my questions about her washroom. To reach it, I climb some stairs (the ceiling is very low), walk down a skinny hall, take a wrong turn that leads to a large room that must be a library: floor to ceiling shelves lined with books, warm light, club chairs, ashtrays. A quick look at the books tells me they are alphabetized. I want to sit in one of the chairs, but am running late for the dog's evening walk and feed so hurry down to the Pumper and my newly fueled up car.

I drive back to the city and the dog, who is dancing around empty food and water bowls; I walk her in the park, then feed her. She sleeps, I sit in an overstuffed arm chair, dip into my staying up late habit, though tonight it is with the variation of being in this strange, at least new, setting.

Two days later, I drop off the dog for her morning grooming appointment, drive back to the gas station. The trip takes longer than I remembered. On my way, it thunderstorms. When I find the gas station, it still thunderstorms. I park, dash inside. There stands the Pumper, smoking, at her cash register. Her hands are wet. She unties a scarf, also wet, to reveal dry, perfectly set hair. I say, I need gas, but no hurry because I must use your restroom, and maybe I could look at your books. She nods. I try to catch her eyes, but they focus on the cash register, and a plug-in calculator next to it. I stand, trying to breath quietly, repeat, I need gas, but there's no hurry, I'll run up to the restroom, and can I maybe peek at those books. She raises her head. There's yellow in her hair, sparkling like sun or a bright star. Her wrists twinkle with bracelets. She scans my dress and hair, suggests we share a light meal.

Wearing the same exercise sandals as DR's sister's, she leads me into the kitchen, makes and butters toast, compliments me on my dress (I say I got it from my sister, without dipping into details). I ask about her books, she says the books belong to her friend who is hiding.

I have questions but must leave and pick up my employer's dog. I tell the Pumper. She fills my tank, says, Sports utility vehicles are impractical. They easily flip, are inefficient to heat and cool, and get poor gas mileage.

Driving home, I think about how working for my employer is different from what I had expected, but not sad. The job gives me opportunities to sit for long periods, uninterrupted. Not that I don't have my responsibilities to see DR, give his sister her messages, walk her dog, care for her home, and co-op.

DR's Sister's co-op has—for this large, dirty city—a spectacular yard. One area is filled with flowering bushes whose cuttings decoratively fill her in and out door urns. Now she is off on global business, it's my responsibility to fill them, a job she knows I'm trained in but don't have shoes for, so she lends me her rubber gardening clogs, as long as I promise to clean them.

They're stored in her hallway closet, rhs, fourth shelf from the top. This is a highly organized closet, filled with leisure gear, located off of a hallway wallpapered in yellow checks. The bathroom next to it—stocked with fragrant body products—is wallpapered in brown checks. Now I'm out on the balcony, sweeping leaves. Peeking through the telescope, I see the Seamstress, draped in hair, holding a fringed handbag, gesturing wildly to two men I've seen on the block. Each holds several fat manila envelopes. Poking out of her fringed bag, too, are several envelopes.

I go out, not to see more of the Seamstress but to walk the dog. Outside I hear her voice rise up, down. Her arms, too, rise up, down.

Several days of dog walking works back the appetite I'd lost during my first days and nights in this new job, when I only drank broth, only ate crumbled crackers.

I somewhat miss my studio apartment, and my job at the

music store; changes in routine, bed, address, and responsibilities, all add up to disruption.

That same day I get hungry I also get a fax from my boss, directing me to enjoy the cans and jars of food filling her basket to the right of her oven. I assemble my first real lunch (canned fish, potatoes, jarred artichokes). After eating it I walk the dog, long and hard, in the park. Footsteps crunch on the ground behind me; it's the Seamstress; her wide brown eyes, their deeply creased lids, her pencil thin figure. She doesn't recognize my employer's dog, or me. We, the dog and I, go home. I clean, air, polish.

The next few days something, maybe food, fills me with energy to work out with DR, and do all the work his sister asks of me. But energy generation doesn't mean all is well. Especially when it is impossible to focus on anything besides exercise and chores. Leaning over my employer's balcony, trying to focus, I scan the street, see men and women enter and exit the Seamstress' building, wonder how many go to see her.

One evening, during this period of unfocused energy (a logical response, DR and I agree, to my new setting), I visit our gym, step on and program a treadmill, look up to see the Seamstress on the machine directly across from me. Walking next to her, a puffy haired, chisel featured man. A tape measure hangs out of his sweat pant pocket.

I finish my treadmill program (1 hour, hills), shower, walk home to DR; he has laid the mini bar with plates of store bought Italian antipasto, and an ice bucket filled with assorted micro brews.

PHYSH

Next morning I speed walk with the dog. In the early afternoon I speed walk without her past a neighborhood university. Across one red-bricked building, a banner advertising a conference on urban culture. Several small groups, wearing badges, stream out the front, double door. I picture the end of participants' day: beverages, handshakes, names and addresses scribbled on sheets of paper. I recognize one person: the puffy haired man who walked next to the Seamstress. He is very handsome. His little left hand clutches a tape measure.

I want to go home; my mouth is dry, my teeth hurt; though I floss and brush regularly.

"Home," brushing my teeth, I catch my reflection in my employer's pretty bathroom mirror. My reflection looks blotchy, puffy, as if sobs have racked me. They haven't racked me. But seeing that face, something unleashes, and now tears do totally flow. I go up to and out on the balcony, fight a small urge to leap off, free flying at last, more seriously consider the telescopes: does my employer use them for professional, or personal reasons? I sweep up the leaves fallen from her trees, store some in a jar, the way she asked me to, for decoration. I hear a bell, shrill and urgent, guess it's the door, wish DR, who understands manners better than me, were here. But it is a fax from my employer, asking about her dog, and reminding me to protect my skin on sunny days with the special face cream I'll find in her brown checked wallpaper bathroom.

Later, the UPS man knocks on my door, asks do I know the Seamstress across the street, and could I give her these packages? I answer, I don't *know* her. He explains the packages are presents. From him. But he wants to be anonymous. I ask, Why not ask our doorman. He answers, That doorman recently suffered a grave loss, and hasn't functioned dependably ever since.

When I next walk through the lobby—with DR and the dog—the bereaved man at the desk hands me several packages, would I, as the UPS man said I would, walk them over to the Seamstress? I tell DR to wait, carry the presents across the street, up a set of clean steps, into the lobby, press a buzzer labeled SEAMSTRESS. Down comes that beautiful little man, tape measure slung over his shoulders; my shoulders cramp, I hand him the packages, run back to DR and his sister's dog, us three walk, *powerfully*.

The next afternoon is mild, sunny. DR dogsits, I return to the gas station, hope to see the Pumper, maybe have a smoke and read her books.

I reach the station, a sign in its window reads CLOSED. I walk out back; there's the Pumper, perched on her rose bush surrounded fence. Balancing practice, she explains, leaping down, scooping up fallen petals, saying she'll use them to make pot pourri. I know, but don't say, that the best petal gathering time for pot pourri is in the morning; these, warm from the sun, will have already lost some fragrance. I do ask how can her rose bushes blossom in fall. She answers, They're not real rose bushes, suggests we take a hike.

We hike, she explains she moved here with her college boyfriend, several years after college, and after living and working in the city. This boyfriend disliked the city; craved a rural life: growing food, smelling foliage, hearing nature.

Using a chunk of the large inheritance left by his aunt, herself a land owner, he buys this piece of property that then held a small cherry orchard (the fruit could be picked and sold), a stream (fish for meals), and an electrically wired cabin. He plants, harvests, hunts with a bow and arrow. And integrates into their new community by joining church, environmental and town council meetings.

That first year the couple turns a profit off of the incubated eggs his aunt orders for them, with instructions: hatch and feed until grown up chickens, then butcher and sell. But they otherwise have trouble: robins eat the cherries, their stream is soiled with sewage, the boyfriend stops wanting sex, intercourse or masturbation.

And he turns vegetarian (leaving her to butcher the chickens), moves out of their feather bed onto a thin floor blanket, starts night-hiking.

He tells her he needs the night hikes to smell, feel, hear nature. He tells her how out at night he finds a special tree; kneels before it, gathers its fallen twigs, presses them beneath his clothes. He tells her, before he smelled one flower, now he has learned to smell individual varieties.

Sometimes he comes home, sleeps soundly. Others he stays outside in his self made camp at their property's edge.

Back at her home, the Pumper asks me to come inside while she assembles food for tonight's cocktail party at her town mayor's.

She stands at a butcher block counter, stamps out rounds

of pastry with a juice glass, wraps them around various prepared refrigerated plates of vegetable and nut fillings. And continues:

One morning, over a platter of fried fish her boyfriend caught the night before in his neighbor's unpolluted stream, he tells her he got accepted to graduate school.

During the weeks before he leaves for graduate school, he installs a disposal, a shower and room air conditioners. He regains interest in eating meat, killing chickens and in sex: intercourse and masturbation.

At this point, two things are true: I want to hear more; I have to drive home. I tell the Pumper. She smiles, says, when I return, we can go to Happy Hour, maybe meet her town's mayor. And I can certainly look at her books.

Getting into the sports utility vehicle, realizing I felt, but no longer feel, sulky, I speed home. When I reach it, there's DR, sitting at a table laid with flowers, iced water, daily papers, twisting a band of string into elaborate bends. The dog, appearing well fed and walked, sleeps beside him. I sit as near to DR as I can, though nothing today has in any way depressed me.

After a few hours I borrow a Fisherman sweater from my employer, and convince DR to go walking—for once without the dog.

We walk long, hard. Back in our building lobby, DR hands the bereaved doorman a powdered cookie. Then hands me one. I take a small bite, give it back, and see my white lipped reflection in his mirror shades.

PHYSH

As a child, I dressed loudly, dreamed of the desert: nursing sick soldiers there, piloting planes, camping out. Now I wear clothes that belonged to my family, or would have belonged to them, and spin my pictures according to realistic situations. For example, this job of house and dogsit. This position is important, I can't let something like the gas pumper, her books, their hiding owner disrupt it. To keep this job, and do well at it, I need a regime; a requirement I'm perhaps unable to impose upon myself. Look at today, for example; I shoved things onto DR.

Both DR and I lost families. I, mine, early one morning. Or remember losing them then. Now one, two, maybe three times daily I replay the scene: mud, ribs, screeches. DR follows a similar pattern, though his pictures are totally different. We work well, keeping each other within a restricted orbit. We don't eat out in family restaurants, or during family times. During family times (holidays, Sunday lunch, five o'clock dinner hour) we stay inside; sometimes DR puts a ring on his thumb and sucks it; others we listen to music; others we wash, iron and mend our clothes.

All my clothes belonged to my family, or could have belonged to them. DR's clothes are important to him, but for different reasons. And he hasn't lost his entire family. He still has that sister.

■

I wake up the next morning, not planning to go to the Pumper's. But, because DR finished my chores yesterday so

SIMPLY SEPARATE PEOPLE

well, and the dog is scheduled for a day-long total body groom I drop her off, drive to the Pumper, find her standing in front of a giant mirror, dressed in a too thin for this cool fall weather Capri pant suit. Trying on outfits for the mayor's next party, she explains, pointing to a bench where I should sit. We discuss some choices in her pile, then I ask, what does she mean when she says her friend who owns all those books is HIDING? This is the first sentence of her answer: Trowt, his floor skimming coat, his rich complex meals, his twinkling nose ring.

The next few minutes is silence, only broken by rustling and scratching sounds of her removing the dainty suit, wrapping a bath sheet underneath her arm pits, lighting a candle. Then she tells me about Trowt.

Trowt, a chef, had been their neighbor in the city. When she and the boyfriend moved to the country, he often visited them to update his rural recipe collection, and to oversee construction on an upstairs addition he was building to store volumes of his expanding book collection. Not that he didn't have room in his massive city apartment. But he wanted a separation from that spectacular dwelling.

She describes some of that spectacular dwelling, starting with the two playrooms; one for games, the other for exercise.

Two walls of his exercise room are windows; there's a skylight, a lap pool, an elaborate stereo system. When Trowt is in depression, she says, he flees into music.

Hanging masks fill an entire wall in the game room; an aluminum and oak-shelving unit (with trays of toys—hammers, cars, balls) fills another. In the room's center, three tables: one for puzzles, one checkers, a third for plastic models of several tiered cakes and other complicated pastries.

As she talks, I'm thinking that bath sheet wrapped below her armpits is an unconventional and attractive shift she could wear to the mayor's in warmer weather, also how fine the bones of her shoulders are.

When I again tune into her, she's describing the room where Trowt spends most of his time in his city apartment, the spacious brown and yellow tiled kitchen. Here he cooks his specialties, which include soufflés, pies with non-fruit fillings, but especially casseroles and stews; things cooked a very long time.

I'm still not listening closely, but looking at those shoulders and waiting to hear the answer to my question—why is Trowt, the book owner, hiding. But then I realize she might be giving the word "hiding" a definition I'm unfamiliar with, and that the Pumper is giving me other, what she considers valuable, information. Like about Trowt's bedroom out here in the country—it's tiny, but wide windows and a high off the floor bed give it an illusion of space. And the allergy that set off his interest in food. He discovered that allergy during a camping for music (his college minor) credit in the woods term. Teachers and students slept in cabins, ate in mess halls, practiced music in forests, on beaches and hills. (One teacher, a gardener, offered a popular seminar on disposable-instrument—using local vegetation—construction.) But Trowt felt too nauseated to do anything out of his bunk. And finally, correctly connected his illness to the oats figuring so prominently in the program's vegetarian menu. After he learned of his allergy, he left music school, and the experimental rock band he played in, to devote his time to his kitchen.

I've devoted some time to the kitchen. Years ago, an influential chef invited me to her home for lectures on cooking. I sat on a floor, crowded with other sitting listeners; standing up chefs gave lectures that for me blurred—I couldn't separate their words individually. That night I went home, channeled my energy by copying addresses from an old to new book, and needlepoint, needle pointing.

Still, that evening deepened my interest in cooking, then chefs. Ever since it, I regularly attend cooking lectures. Now here I sit, listen to a story about a chef.

I tune back in. The Pumper is speaking fast and monotone about Trowt, whose food allergy led to an interest in cooking that led to an interest in cookbooks that led to an interest in other books. Browsing for them, collecting them. But he spent so much time with the volumes of non-cookbooks filling up the shelves of his apartment, he got distracted from cooking. So he asked the Pumper and her boyfriend, could he build a library out in their country house? This is the comfortable seeming room lined with books, filled with chairs I saw on my first visit to the bathroom. Trowt visited them frequently. She would pick him up at the station; he'd step off the train, lanky, erect, well nourished, carrying a wax paper lined hatbox filled with fresh baked cookies or individual pies. Mornings he'd be with his books, afternoons out in the fields, forming ideas for new rural recipes, evenings he'd cook up his ideas (walnut creams, stewed chickens). Nights, back up with his books. At some point in his looking at books, he discovered a family secret. And asked a family member about it. The member, gripping Trowt's shoulders, begged, then ordered, Trowt never to mention the secret, just to let the secret go. Trowt said he couldn't promise. The family member digging fingers deep, deeper into Trowt's shoulders, insisted. Trowt reiterated No. Now, he is traveling, which the Pumper believes is a form of hiding. Or this is what the Pumper tells me Trowt's story to her and her boyfriend is. Anyway, she says, Maybe he isn't hiding, maybe he has disappeared.

Now she would like to change the subject because this one depresses her.

She tells me my face looks blotchy, puffy, as if sobs have racked me. I tell her they have not racked me, but I'm having an allergic reaction to face cream my employer suggested I use to protect my face when doing the outdoor work (gardening, dog walking, balcony maintenance) she asks of me. And that I have to go get the dog.

I leave, drive miles in the wrong direction. Reach the edge of a town with a harbor. I hope to see black ships or schooners, but see houses and family crafts. A wooden bridge links that piece of land to an island. On the island stands a neon-lit fortress, topped by a flashing EAT sign .

SIMPLY SEPARATE PEOPLE

I'd heard about the delicious rural food served by this eatery that stands halfway up a steep hill, and has a boatman row customers not opting to take the bridge across. I see the boatman's trailer, the bell hanging from it; a large family now ringing it. He (BOATMAN is emblazoned across his yellow raincoat's back) emerges, points to a billboard announcing today's dinner: roast goose and sweet onion soup, squash. When they nod, he leads them onto his boat, rows them over to the tree filled island.

I'm interested but more than that upset. All this time I could have spent with the Pumper; I worry I was rude to her, leaving so abruptly. Getting out a map, I read it, plot my course and turn "home."

Driving home, I'm remembering a recent telephone conversation with DR's sister a little guiltily. She asked, Have I met the Seamstress. I answer, No, without telling her how much time I've been spending in the country. She tells me the Seamstress has a beautiful assistant, and describes him: short, small hands, puffy hair. On top of working for the Seamstress, he makes hats according to seasonal foliage: spring hats sport tulips; summer ones sport sunflowers. Now it's fall he'll use some burnished red and gold leaf theme, and might borrow from some of the flowering bushes in her co-op's yard, or even from the jars and urns on her balcony. I must not be afraid if he approaches me.

Home, having picked up the dog, and just walked into the door, the phone rings. It is my employer. She asks how I'm eating. When I tell her about the jars and cans of food, and thank her for them, she sounds happy, but emphasizes I should not substitute them for fresh meals.

Which motivates me to go buy and stew a chicken. I season it with spices DR's sister stores in test tubes on a rack mounted above her stove. As I prepare the chicken, I remember the Pumper has plastic herb trays along her kitchen windowsills, and think that would go well with DR's sister's country style decorations. Maybe we'll grow closer and I'll be in a position to tell her. Also, I think how when I hear cooking lectures words blur; I can't separate them individually. So I focus on the speaker's shoes, hair, saliva.

Standing in front of a full-length mirror, I examine my own shoes, hair, and saliva. I can't remember if my shoes actually belonged to my sister; I'm certain they would have belonged to her. My waist length, *Sunflowers* colored hair is in a single braid. My mouth feels void of saliva, in fact very dry, signaling it's time for drinking water.

Heading to the kitchen for water, and to add vegetables to the chicken I'm stewing, I think about this job, its comfortable setting, its sports utility vehicle, its telescopes. Its location across the street from the Seamstress. And how I wasn't totally straight with DR's sister about the Seamstress. How I use her telescope enough to know the Seamstress and her workers' hours (noon to late evening) and am familiar enough with their faces that I recognize them in parks, delis, gas stations.

In the bathroom, I remember last week on the noon dog walk route (around the park's edge, not through it) I'm

SIMPLY SEPARATE PEOPLE

stopped, standing, letting the dog sniff some foliage. Stones crunch behind me; it's the Seamstress walking alone: head low; strides long.

Now I go up to and out on the balcony, polish the weathervane's rooster, consider my feelings toward sewing. I fear the discipline. I know a little knowledge can turn someone who doesn't sew into someone who can. Still, I fear that discipline.

Other handwork does not frighten me. I enjoy embroidery, even repaired the ottoman DR's sister gave me quite easily.

Finally it's evening and time to dog-walk. Who knows where DR has decided to go today? But we have an appointment in two hours to meet at the gym. The dog and I walk. On our way back we see a manila envelope lying on the sidewalk in front of the Seamstress' building. I pick it up, peek inside. Wallet sized snapshots of dresses on mannequins paper-clipped to thin intricately diagrammed paper. I have to believe they're patterns, and that I should return them to the Seamstress, or one of her crew. The dog and I enter her building. The doorman tells me he's just back from vacation, and that dogs are not allowed. I show him what I've found, explain who I think it belongs to. He agrees, says it is great to be back here after vacation, and that he'll return the pattern-filled envelope to someone at the Seamstress'. I ask him, does he know DR's sister's doorman who works in the building across the street. He nods his head. All smiles leave his face.

He tells me that doorman recently suffered a grave loss, and maybe someday will want to vacation but for now is best off sticking to a strict routine.

DR and I stick to routines. We both lost our families (though he still has that sister), so much got disrupted; I think we now exaggerate routine's importance. We are strict about going to the gym, and going to work, even when we feel sick. We have our separate times, like when I go see the Pumper, sweep his sister's balcony, or use her telescopes to view the Seamstress and her employees. And with my new job and eating situation, our eating patterns had to be re-established. First I could not eat, then we had take out and canned foods, now I'm stewing a chicken.

Having dropped off the manila envelope, I have an hour before I meet DR at the gym. Since I've lived at his sister's, we work out less often in the mornings. Once home, I see he's left laundry (most of it, sticky pajama bottoms), so wash them with a load of my own.

After our gym work-out, DR changes into a shirt I find upsetting: patterns of uncomfortably twisting giraffes, on unpleasant, nylon material.

Home, eating chicken, we get a fax from his sister, reminding us to pay kind, non-invasive attention to the doorman. Also to allow the Seamstress' beautiful assistant free access to her balcony foliage. A good time for me to tell DR about my sewing fears, something I don't think he knows about me. His answer: View the discipline from a distance; the running stitch, called basting, joins two pieces of fabric together *temporarily* ... I can't remember his other examples because I could not listen closely.

People have different weak points: pets, mean sex, candy. Mine are overexplaining, and not listening closely. Sometimes I can but often words blur; I can't separate them individually. Those cooking lectures, for example, or the times I can't understand DR.

PUMPER

*N*ever respond recklessly, my scientist parents taught my brothers and me.

Work hard, elicit accurate, if necessary complex, information; a smell or appearance we welcome doesn't signal safe; a plant or animal repulsive to us can, but doesn't certainly, mean danger. Reactions—quick gulps of comprehension—to anything, they taught, only leads to a hollow grasp, if not complete misunderstanding, of the subject.

The boyfriend I had for a long time, though not a scientist, believed in operating this way too, which was maybe what brought us together, and kept us there during college, after college and through his first graduate degree. Then things blurred; for years we had sporadic cordial, sometimes sexual, encounters with a mutual understanding we weren't "together." I'm writing this down to get him out of my skin. I just started sweating now, writing about him. Before this I wrote two letters, served two customers (I operate a gas/service station), copied a recipe without perspiration. Now I'm sweating and the temperature hasn't changed, neither have my clothes or the amount of food and drink in my stomach; all that has changed is I'm writing about him. It's like my body acts: detoxify.

Or, as I learned on a recent daylong meditation course, perspiration can signal rebirth.

It's funny, that boyfriend sticking with me, especially since I'm in love with someone else, a person who has disappeared.

Back to that boyfriend: I met him in college, in the basement of the library where I went to study, meet friends and eat. I had a condition in college (it ended when I left); I couldn't eat unless I was around a lot of not-eating people. I couldn't eat in my room, when I was alone. I couldn't eat in restaurants or in the dorm cafeteria with everyone eating. I could only eat in situations, which were crowded with non-eaters: buses, sidewalks, and lobbies. I didn't mind when people ate, that never irritated me; it only left me unable to eat. Nibbling didn't bother me. I ate around nibblers, people nibbling small bags of peanuts, caramels, crackers; library vending machine food. I met this boyfriend at a library vending machine. I had just bought a package of vanilla cream sandwich cookies; he a package of sunflower seeds (unsalted). He carried a textbook titled POPULAR CUL-

TURE. I asked about this and his answer (to paraphrase): TV, fashion, celebrities, these things offered fertile thinking ground. But ultimately our approach (*how* we read something) is potentially more significant than *what* we read.

OK. A message similar, without being identical, to what my parents taught me. He was curious, attractive, somewhat sexual.

Now, years later, I'm living out in the country in a building and plot of land he bought and owns (the gas/service station is my personal addition). He went through a period of wanting to experience country living. Now he has gotten several graduate degrees and is off traveling globally. I'm here, waiting, not for him but for Trowt, the man I love. He has disappeared.

I'm very busy out here in the country: running a gas station, monitoring residents and visitors, working in my garden, researching projects for our town mayor, also socializing with him, his remarkable partner the Seamstress, and their colorful weekend guests.

Reading Trowt's books, examining his clothes.

My boyfriend left me well provided for financially, thanks to what he did with money left to him by his famous ballerina mother, and his aunt.

Thinking of Trowt is painful, I don't know where he is or if he'll ever come back. I can't bear to picture him too graphically. Instead of picturing his big chest or face, I recall less charged physical features: the hair on his forearms, the nails of his well formed fingers.

SIMPLY SEPARATE PEOPLE

After college, my boyfriend and I lived in the city, where I was happy (perspiration starts again now). I had a big salary, big office, big desk, big set of windows. A big budget for a big wardrobe. I loved my job (research on consumer shopping trends). I loved my friends, my gym, the places where you could see movies and eat dinner. But my boyfriend grew grumpy with city life, with what he called its artificiality. I did things that understandably irritated him, like staying late at work, and spending a lot of time at the gym. He said I over worked and exercised. And he disliked my interest in fashion; especially the high heels that he forecasted would deform my feet. That's when he'd question my values, very rightly describe me as ambitious and vain. He disliked my habit of going to my office at night to finish something, or find an answer for a project-in-process, saying that it was unhealthy that I couldn't sleep with unanswered questions floating around my head. On that schedule, I went into work later the next day (a treat for me, never—like my brothers and parents—an early riser).

My friendship with Trowt deepened during those late mornings because I tasted and judged his newly concocted breakfast breads and juices.

City life was busy, not stressful. I didn't just visit my gym to exercise; that facility offered complex equipment, classes, people and energy bars and beverages. For me, life in the city was interesting the way a movie was. I didn't have to work hard to find things interesting, the way I did in college or the way I do now, out here in the country. Not that excitement searching can't provide its own brand of rewards.

My boyfriend enjoyed his job there, teaching English as a second language. He had time for hobbies: sports, relaxation, gardening (he tended his leased plot, a few blocks away from our apartment, in a community garden). At night, he and his friends played baseball or did a group meditation, then sat around drinking tea, or beer. But he craved a quieter routine. His reasons for wanting to move out of the city had nothing to do with career failure.

My parents are fortunate to be so fascinated by science. My fascination is less respectable; it is with people. Keeping track of people; how they dress, talk, wear their hair. Ways people spend their work and free time. I've done this for excellent pay, but it is also my hobby.

Trowt. He aroused me, without inflaming my curiosity (highly unusual response from me, personally).

Trowt. As much as I hope writing this gets that boyfriend out of my skin, I hope Trowt will permeate it. I'll start back: Our next door neighbor in the city was a chef named Trowt. The first time I saw him he was removing a soufflé from the oven with two green checked pot holders. I meant to knock on his door to introduce myself, but his door was not only unlocked, it stood wide open. I stood in the entrance, watching a large, limber frame leap across a spacious kitchen (neighboring a living room packed with toys; *that* I'll describe in detail later), pick up the green checked potholders, open the oven, remove a soufflé. I thought we were alone until I saw a group of three onlookers, wearing aprons. Trowt, too, wore an apron. I introduced myself as the new neighbor, he responded briefly, enthusiastically, explaining he was teaching a soufflé seminar. Would I like to hear the finishing comments he couldn't put off for too long since they referred to a soufflé, fresh from the oven? I nodded, staring at his eyelashes. He explained what to look for in a soufflé, fresh from the oven, waving his fingers over its top and sides, spooning out servings, introducing himself and his students, and asking politely about my boyfriend and me.

Why am I recounting now? I think the influence of Physh, the Pet/House Sitter, who stopped for gas and who saw and got interested in Trowt's books. We've become friends. She visits, talks, gets me to talk. She talks, without overtalking. She says I get her to talk—something I've been told before. I haven't yet told her about my project with the Seamstress and our mayor, but sense that I could.

Enough recounting for now. Time to bake.

■

I like our small town, especially our mayor. He's getting older but I have confidence he'll live a long time. When he put on a few pounds, I led him through a series of reducing exercises which included aerobic activity and yoga. (His partner, the frighteningly fit Seamstress supported me wholeheartedly.) I practiced yoga in the city, and it is a big part of my life out here. It was something I shared with Trowt, something I haven't yet mentioned to Physh. I believe in another life in which the mayor and I were somehow connected. Brother and sister? We share deep affection, but no sexual electricity. The sexual electricity between him and the Seamstress is *something*.

He gives a lot of cocktail parties these days, and weekend gatherings which people, some celebrities even, fly in for. It's a total world he's created at his estate. Much of its success is thanks to the Seamstress; his personality and his community project have both improved immensely since her consistent involvement. His weekend gatherings help me advance my cooking practice; the Seamstress and mayor fly in celebrity chefs. I like celebrity chefs; they don't make me feel artificial. Some of the non-celebrity (I guess you'd say non-high-profile) chefs make me feel that way. Like I'm artificial for wanting to eat low-fat (engaging in occasional special event high-fat blowouts) and hoping when I see myself in a mirror I look trim. My old boyfriend would say, though, there aren't differences between the two kinds of chefs, and I'm only projecting the way I view myself onto them.

He (the mayor) has quite a past; he was and is well connected. Hooked into high profile personalities. But chooses to stay out here in the country in his activity filled estate house, its endless grounds. Pools (indoor and outdoor) stables, beauty salons, beaches, fields, mountains, restaurants, gardens, big screen TVs. Hiking trails, pets, child care. The Seamstress helped him plan it. Even when I slip into one of my shadowy, depressive moods, the environment created by his estate pumps me up. Not in any long-term way. I have to rely on other things for that. But quick fixes can be useful. I've made some mistakes at the mayor's. With the sweater store owner, for example, revealing what some perceive as my personal problem to him. Our town is out in the country, but several people, besides the mayor, have estates here. So the economy supports a selection of specialty stores. People from the city even drive here to buy specialty items, and write articles about the food, clothes, used books and furniture customers can buy. Anyway, there is a celebrated sweater store out here. Its owner is a brooding, heavy drinker with amazing legs (he wears shorts except on bitter cold days) and abdominal muscles (those I first saw during a mayor-sponsored pool party).

I had seen him several times, and consistently found him interesting personally and sexually. I visited his store, and became at once aroused and shy, hiding behind several wide hatted heads, customers buying up sweaters. At the mayor sponsored pool party we were introduced, we danced; he asked me to come to his home above his sweater store. We entered his living room, filled with aquariums and rugs, and started kissing. But I wanted his story: Why sweaters, why here, did he learn knitting from someone in his family? In return, he related a deeply moving story. At its end, he wanted to give me a sweater to thank me for both opening him up and constructively listening. We walk downstairs into the shop, choose a sweater, go back upstairs. But by that time I want to leave. See this is part of what some perceive of as my problem: usually information, not physical contact, arouses me. Once my curiosity is sated, I'm physically unresponsive.

People put all sorts of things between themselves and intimacy: food, drugs, excess weight, clutter. I understand, information is my personal choice for a cushion. Which is why Trowt is crucial: he doesn't fit this pattern; he doesn't make me curious; doesn't inspire me to elicit information. Him, I just wanted to experience, to take in. My boyfriend was another story, I'm not articulating this well. More later. I'm not in a sweat mood.

After that night, things were sometimes awkward with the sweater storeowner, and I couldn't bring myself to wear the sweater he gave me, though it was beautiful. Once after a night of heavy drinking he spat "TEASE" in my ear, but soon things settled into friendly. This is one of the advantages of our community structured by our mayor; there's nothing permanent as far as grudges or bad blood goes. It doesn't hurt that shortly after that the sweater storeowner met a breathtaking Italian movie star who remains his steady girlfriend.

The mayor's estate brings culture into this small town, and brings the people living here together. I have figured out a way to learn a lot about people and keep a steady income: the gas/service station. I don't need income now, my boyfriend left me well taken care of, but I am saving for later.

Why does mentioning my boyfriend cause this unpleasant perspiration? Look how physically comfortable he left me: house, money, a life I enjoy. All these things are true. Still, something about him gives me the creeps toward myself. Something about him makes me sick with myself.

I like living out here, though I miss the city. The city is electric; eclectic, bustling. You can be anonymous. Here everyone knows you. Even the weekend crowds include some regulars. When my boyfriend lived here, we decided to isolate. We only knew the mayor through our organic farming research. His cats sometimes visited, and we were invited to, but didn't attend, his parties. Why go to parties here? We rationalized; if we wanted parties, we'd go back to the city. We kept to ourselves, and participated in community religious and recycling groups. We worked, did not socialize. When he left for graduate school, I found, and hung with, a different group of people, starting with the mayor, the Seamstress, their guests and chefs.

I'm boring myself writing this. I want to spice things up, without lying. Lies have their own momentum; once you start, you can't stop.

All I really want to think about is Trowt; an urge that takes some resisting.

When we lived in the city, I took Trowt for granted. I loved Trowt; he didn't make me curious. He was our neighbor: radiant, maternal, well fed. Sexual. When my boyfriend first mentioned moving, Trowt suggested staying with us, part time, in our country house. My boyfriend had been given a plot of land by his aunt, who was very good friends with the town mayor. I loved my boyfriend, but wouldn't have been so excited about the move if Trowt hadn't come.

PUMPER

The hairs on his well formed fingers.

This is how Trowt could be. When I asked why he wanted to visit us in the country, he answered: To store some belongings. To invent new recipes. And, added, with a smile, Tension is a wonderful source of creativity. My heart soared, hoping he meant us; our unresolved sexual tension. But later I realized he could have meant the tension he sensed between me and my boyfriend, or the tension of being outside the city; it's *tense* being out of the city. It takes time to mend a fence, fix a toilet, reerect a pole. There aren't 10:00 morning movies or 24 HR stores selling yogurt, rice, chocolate. I don't live far from the city, and sometimes travel there. And go to the weekends at the mayor's, which gives me the taste of the city. But all without Trowt. I briefly mentioned his books and clothes. Trowt stores his well stocked library here, also his extensive, complex clothing collection—he constructed some of the sportier pieces himself. The library is upstairs, his closet is just off to its side. Many evenings, I sit in his library club chairs, read his books; sit in his room sized closet, finger the folds of his suits, sweaters, ties. I plan to pick out a selection from his wardrobe, and have it altered to fit me.

In truth, I don't drive into the city anymore. I used to. But leaving home is nerve wracking, and all I do in the city is think I see Trowt. I'm not proud of this but it is true. And I am *very busy* here, in the country.

I skipped two grades in elementary school. I was a good student but emotionally immature. I had a reading problem, but understood mathematics.

SIMPLY SEPARATE PEOPLE

I had the patience, and stamina, to spend a long time with initially unsolvable problems.

Still my case, the difference is it's now with people, not numbers.

The mayor, responding to the glut of money and culture in the city, the devastation of our physical environment, while also capitalizing on the fact people love the country, but don't know what to do there, expanded his estate to establish—with his partner the Seamstress—a fabulously virtual environment. This explains his constantly blooming rose bushes, joyful, beautiful, artificial. His estate has developed into an adult activity ground.

Many people who excel in an area have a Significant Other. A muse. A partner, maybe sexual, maybe a great fan or advisor. I like to think I had something to do with Trowt's development.

And if I did not, well, I believe self delusions can be very positive.

And I said earlier, lies can be traps that generate frightening momentum. Yet there is also the possibility that something general, even precious, can come from lies.

I will tell you one thing that is no lie: the varicose veins in Trowt's legs are extreme.

■

I sat down to write about me, my boyfriend and Trowt, to explain why I stayed out here, starting my own brand of research detection, my lucrative gas/service station. Yet, things pop up from childhood. For instance, when a boy in 2nd

PUMPER

grade, Ian, kept shoving me, I told our teacher who took me aside, smiled, and whispered, "It's because he *likes* you." Also about bad things I've done. Not just with the sweater store owner either. Recently, I asked him about his muscular legs and abdominals. He told me the program which works for him: Run 1 hour every morning in good weather; ride his stationary bike that long when conditions outside are poor, and do 1,000 sit-ups regardless. 1,000 sit-ups. He drinks heavily but only gin or lite beer. And no deep-fried food, though he uses olive oil and ghee liberally. He's late middle aged. For being late middle aged, his body is astounding. He is balding, but his body is astounding. He is short. I thought he was tan but learned that he has natural dark skin tone. As I said, he usually wears shorts, which I appreciate because it allows a view of his legs: two trunks of shapely muscle. There are two kinds of male builds I'm personally attracted to. The willowy and well toned frame (men with these builds often have a hunched over posture), and the sturdy, tree trunk frame (these men tend not to be physically limber). The sweater storeowner is the second. Trowt is the first, though he has excellent posture. Maybe his varicose veins came from standing so long in kitchens, but might also have come from genetics.

My boyfriend was thin, un-muscular.

I like to think I had some influence on Trowt. Not that he ever confided in me, like: Let me talk to you and only you . . .

Once we prepared an entire meal of aphrodisiac oriented food.

■

I'm starting recounting again in the morning, before too many things happen to form an impression.

Something just happened which formed an impression. I served an early morning customer needing gas, an oil change and information. He drove out here from the city, explaining he came back early from a sabbatical because so much random crime occurred in the country he visited to live and study in. Crime, he himself experienced at his *bank*. Deposited money in an account he'd opened for the sabbatical term, and the next day got a threatening, anonymous note from someone demanding exactly that amount of money. Someone at the bank had leaked information. Or, somehow seen his bank statement. The situation terrified him. He withdrew his money, cut short his sabbatical and rushed "home." But had sublet his apartment. So will spend some time out here, in the country; do I know of a room? I send him to the mayor's.

What I notice, and mentally file away: blinding white, yet uneven, teeth (perhaps he bleaches them excessively), thick gold wedding band, running shoes. Next to him on the seat: a well worn, large backpack, a fine leather brief case. A tape deck plays what sounds like folk music. The singing, chant like, is in a language I don't recognize.

See how much I learn, pumping gas? When I'm pumping gas, or servicing a car, I look inside each vehicle, explore evidence as closely as my boyfriend did his favorite tree, its many holes and branches. In this way, I channel my urge of curiosity; offset the urge to get satisfaction inelegantly, for example, ogling people in public, or staring inside their windows.

I miss the city. But will not return without Trowt.

How I got more connected with my college boyfriend, after meeting him and his Popular Culture textbook, was this: I had taken a term off from school to earn money waitressing (a profession which, like my gas/service station, generates income and allows people investigation at once). Since I was around customers eating so much in the restaurant (*and* staff wolfing down snacks in the kitchen, or enjoying meals on an employee card table set up in a small room behind the kitchen) I couldn't eat. It was winter, too freezing to eat outside. Home was no good either, since I lived alone. I'd been using vending machines in lobbies of hotels, train and bus stations, the college lecture hall buildings. This evening I wanted to go to the library, where I could consume food with the studiers and nibblers, but since I wasn't enrolled I didn't have a valid student identification card so couldn't enter the library, my favorite place to eat.

I also needed to look up something one of my good tipping customers mentioned and I pretended I understood, but didn't really.

My pockets, filled with change from waitressing (because of my dependence on vending machines, I didn't turn mine in for bills like the other staff), were heavy. I stood, shivering, outside the library, looking down its many steps, hoping to run into a student I knew who could bring me inside as a guest on her student id. There he jogged—he who would be

SIMPLY SEPARATE PEOPLE

my boyfriend—two steps at a time, wearing a pointed knit hat with attached earflaps, jeans, lace up boots and a canvas chore jacket. We said, "Hi, haven't seen each other for awhile" simultaneously. He tells me about his term paper; I tell him I hope to look something up in one of the library encyclopedias, but cannot get in without a valid student identification card, which I don't have since I'm not a current student. He invites me in.

Inside, he heads for a study carrel (near the encyclopedias), I to the vending machines. Surrounded by students sipping, crunching, I put in my coins, get the carton of milk, the packet of cheese crackers. I drink the milk, start on the crackers, walk over to the encyclopedias near my boyfriend's carrel (well, boyfriend-to-be). He's sitting hunched over, having no trouble getting immediately absorbed in his books. No nibbling, no browsing through a glossy magazine first, nothing. Immediate absorption. Wish that could be my style. He saved the carrel next to him for me.

Now. While we went out for two years in this small western town during college (how we handled my eating condition is another story itself), and then moved east to the city where I became infatuated with high profile people and fashion (and regained my ability to eat any time any where, except movie theaters and subways, where people shouldn't eat anyway), what I did next explains why he thought I was serious and why he ever suggested we move to this plot of the land in the country, the plot of land he no longer lives on but I still do. Because of a story one of my better tipping customers told me, I looked up Homesteading. The Homestead Law; the Homestead Act.

Here's the definition: (Webster's New World 1992) "... in US history, an act of Congress 1862 to encourage settlement of land in the west by offering 160 acre/65 hectare plots cheaply or even free to those willing to cultivate and improve the land for a stipulated amount of time ... some still available today."

Seeing my research topic, he drew closer. Homesteading was his fantasy; educated city dwellers leaving "that success" for some closer to earth and spirit experience was his personal ambition.

I'm sweating, faced with the fact that my looking up The Homestead Act set my boyfriend and me on a weak foundation—dishonesty—from the start.

I did not look up The Homestead Act out of personal interest, I looked it up—as I said—because one of my better tipping customers was discussing this with me and rather than ask him what it meant—being sensitive, as, perhaps, some other educated wait staff are—about my intelligence, I went along with his conversation, pretending I understood the Homestead concept. If I had looked up areas that truly interested me (couture, confection, spy cameras, strength training), I doubt I would have seduced that boyfriend. Lies have their individual momentum.

SEAMSTRESS

I, have spent the last two decades making clothes, accessories, dishes and beds for humans and pets. Now, that business lucrative, my reputation sound, I'm branching out, collaborating on a project which incorporates interior and exterior design with assorted leisure and work.

My design terrain is the conceptual/visual: interplaying bodies with what adorns them when working, socializing, exercising. Just as a writer sets the tone of a "Thank You for Your Sympathy" card; or a speaker determines the pitch of communication used to insist on dietary restrictions when ordering lunch in a serious restaurant; so can an outfit wearer shape clothing's expression.

I work slowly. It takes time for me to get an idea, to find the proper fabric. Then to cut a pattern, baste material, pin it

SEAMSTRESS

on a model or mannequin. I had solid, informal, training as a seamstress, first from my childhood nanny/tutor (we called her Nantor) then years later from my childrens' grandmother, Rhulera.

Until I was 6, my musical brother Selmon 8, our family lived in one large, cosmopolitan city. Then my mother died of a sudden illness, brutally debilitating our father emotionally. He couldn't stay in our house, even in our city, with so many things reminding him of mom, so requested a company transfer, requiring global travel. His new job landed him in cities anywhere from a few days to a month. Wanting Selmon and me to stay with him, he planned on hiring two staff people: a babysitter and a tutor, but got both in one person: Nantor. Nantor turned out to be a gifted seamstress and cook, as well as a big hearted, sturdily educated person; we learned foundations of cooking and sewing, along with history, grammar and math. We dressed well (she made most of our clothes, but not dad's suits), and ate different foods than mom cooked, something crucial for getting dad to eat. Our house smelled like tomatoes, coffee and cinnamon, ingredients mom hadn't focused on. After a few years, dad calmed down enough to settle. I still picture Selmon and me taking the bus, or walking, home from school, seeing Nantor stand outside our house, wearing boots or slippers, depending on the weather, looking down at the ground or up at the sky. She'd take our hands, walk us inside, feed us a snack, ask (except for the year we went to a uniform-requiring school): what our teachers wore; what our classmates wore; what we ate for lunch; what had been that day's most interesting and most boring lessons. Afterwards, we did homework, then helped her in the kitchen. When dad came home he'd take his evening swim, eat with us, help us with homework. Then he'd go in his study, while Selmon and I went in Nantor's sewing room, to do stitching exercises on diversely shaped patches of cloth. Even then, my musical brother excelled at cooking, I at sewing. He, now a chef, attributes his cooking strategies and style—preference for sauces, stews, things cooked a very long time—to Nantor, and I likewise connect my design sensibility to her; particularly, the tenderness I try to infuse in my lines, and my dislike of things too neat. You won't find head to toe designs, or closely matching pieces, in my constructions. Nantor, who believes in learning skills from the inside out, taught me how to find the magic in a great piece of clothing: unstitch, then re-stitch it. We did this on separates bought at flea markets and end of the year store sales.

I am no design genius. My strength is practicality; the clothes I make are feminine, comfortable, easy; these words might evoke ordinary-casual, but I stress body curves and parts. For women, I use sweaters, shirts and jackets just a little too big, as though borrowed, but generally pair these pieces with plunging necklines, short skirts, midriffs; separates which show skin. And my evening lines are body hugging. I work with natural materials: wool, silk, leather; and lately I'm mixing them with some of the new high-tech metallic fabrics. I use obviously fake stuff like diamonds or furs, because they convey humor so effectively, but wouldn't use a "realistic" fake fiber such as polyester made to look like wool.

Fashion blends commerce with art. My talented peers do not generate big income from their brilliant designs, but from low cost items that sell abundantly: underwear, fragrances, t-shirts. The first income I generated came from work I did with city police, creating armored dog vests for police dog crews. I then put those earnings toward developing profitable lines of casual belts, fitness shoes, and pet clothing and utensils. I don't mean humiliating jackets or booties for pets. Just functional scarves and sweaters for blustery, cold; interesting collars; leashes that are friendly to the walkers' hand and wrist; bowls that won't tip over when a pet eats or laps; and droppers and spoons for medicine, vitamins or treats. When my own pet suddenly, violently, died, I couldn't continue the line (also by that time, did not need to financially), so sold it to a young company started by one of my previous employees.

The most brilliant designers fuse bits of history and contemporary culture with irony and glamour. One gifted colleague of mine made a series of lines influenced by an athletic style of dance involving lifts and throws. Her pieces tapped into notions of identity and expression, using images of heavy and light in a way that was shriekingly genius (note: her profits came from the perfume, dance-like shoes and assorted tights and leggings she made to accompany the line, not the dazzling line itself). Another fashion genius I know combines prints on delicate, sheer material, with stark colors in heavy, flat fabric, resulting in an exquisite blend of hardened and fragile. That isn't me. My work isn't abstract, because my abilities don't lie there. My abilities lie in defining subtle, almost diary-like differences of fairly obvious emotion. Take, for example, two successful lines of my relaxed cotton trousers. One I developed for a subject to sit in while contemplating a friend in a non-sexual way. The second line, tighter fitting, and made out of more delicate material, is for that same individual to wear when contemplating someone in a passionate, desire-infused way.

The difference between those experiences is great; the difference between the two pairs of pants is slight, subtle, and infinitely fascinating to me.

That is my professional past. Presently, I'm out in the country, planning an adventure community with a colleague I spent months trying not to become physically attracted to. Physical attraction is a decision, not a four-wheel vehicle with no brake mechanism, I told myself. But then I learned his feelings toward me were also highly charged.

The entertainment complex is located in a small country town, my colleague is the town's mayor.

I wouldn't doubt this change—from clothes and accessories to collaboration with the mayor—started when I started to wrinkle. Wrinkles don't bother me aesthetically; they illustrate my history, its thrills and mistakes. My wrinkles are not unattractive, however they do drive home the fact that my days are numbered. And tragically losing my pet drove that home too.

SEAMSTRESS

Working hard on new projects is a good distraction from personal problems, and some of those have cropped up recently. Years before, I started and left behind a family. If you want to judge me negatively, do. But no one is harsher on me than me, and I only left after making sure everyone was safe, loved and over-all provided for.

As I mentioned, because of my mother's death and my father's profession, we—Selmon and I—grew up globally, living in different cosmopolitan cities, many overlooking rivers, lakes and oceans, experiences I took for granted until I went to college in a small, landlocked town (fields, horses, barbed-wire fences), and fell forcefully in love with its big meals, big spaces, and, the big men who grew up there. One big man anyway.

My brother and I left home for college the same year. I started college one year early; Selmon, who played in a popular local band, started one year late. Our departure was hard on dad and Nantor, who encouraged us to study away from home, but at the same time, enjoyed us nearby. Selmon's exit saddened them enough, but at least he was going to school in a place we were familiar with (and had even *lived* in for short periods of time). My departure not only saddened, but deeply worried, them for one pregnant reason: they were anti-rural region. Those zones, they then believed, were homogenous, uneducated and violent. Later in life, they would live happily in small, country communities, but at this point they were anti-rural region.

Selmon left one week before I did. We were all excited in

the car on the way to the airport, singing, clapping, joking, but we cried when he boarded the plane, and the three of us drove home silent. The next day I got a letter from my college, written by someone named Bry, explaining she had been assigned as my Big Sister. Our college, she wrote, had a Big Brother/Big Sister program for incoming freshmen. A same-sex older student to help newcomers in the emotional and practical needs of the college orientation process. The letter from Bry had a warm, friendly tone as she explained she was a child psychology major (specializing in early childhood development), had grown up in the college town, and planned to open an alternative elementary school there after graduating, she looks forward to meeting me, will be there if I need her, etc. The friendly, informative communication was so nice, it couldn't help but ease dad and Nantor's anxiety when they took me to the airport the next week, though, they were still more subdued than when we took Selmon.

Just before I boarded the plane, Nantor whispered, with a short laugh, she hoped me studying in a rural region would knock any notions of long term living there out of my system. Then went on to say, tears filling her eyes, Please be careful, adding that she knew I'd learn valuable lessons, she only hoped not at too great cost.

My first night at college I caught the airport shuttle to my dormitory room, where I met Bry—tall and beautiful—who told me I had a double room to myself, because my would-be roommate had unenrolled. The college never replaced her, so I was alone in that double room the whole year. Bry took me to a party with other incoming freshman and their Big Sisters and Big Brothers, and we all went to a restaurant that served plates piled with immense portions of food, and seemed to be full of handsome boys and men wearing boots.

The next week, one of these boys in boots turned up in my math class. His name: Euge.

Math was a strong subject for both of us, and we became friendly when our teacher asked us to tutor some of the MC (mathematically challenged) students.

My Big Sister Bry was, surprising to me, one of my MC students. I learned quickly that she had no problems with math, as long as she moved along at her individual pace. Together we made excellent progress; I adored her.

Euge was on the college football team, but had broken an ankle breaking a horse (one of his family's many businesses was raising horses) so had extra time for math, not being able to ride (except leisurely) or play football. Maybe this also gave him extra time to date, because he asked me on one.

On our first date we went to a college football game he would have starred in had his ankle not broken, then sat outside, looking at open fields and sky, talking. We were physically exotic to one another. He: huge, pale, strong; I: tiny, dark, "heady" (his words). "You are so heady," he used to say, explaining later that meant smart. I know a lot of people besides me have this experience when recalling young loves: you think back, trying to capture the dizzy rapture, but there are impediments, usually connected with things happening after the dizzy rapture. Dizzy rapture's aftermath. It is sometimes difficult to think of things that are sweet, when sad things that follow bleed into them.

Which, I know, means re-thinking pinning those sorts of value judgments to experiences in the first place.

Euge and I spent months in dizzy rapture: sex, lemonade, leisurely horse rides. He lived at home, but the double-dorm room I had to myself gave us privacy.

At his mother's suggestion, with the help of a neighbor, and my total support, he switched horse training tactics from horse breaking to horse whispering.

Meeting his extraordinary mother, Rhulera, only enhanced my breathy, nearly all encompassing attraction for Euge.

Rhulera, in a coincidence too great for me to ignore, was, similar to Nantor, a seamstress and cook. Unlike Nantor, she had turned both abilities into highly lucrative businesses.

She had started a food specialty business out of her home, now located in town and managed by her oldest son, a businessman trained as a chef, which exported her recipes of local delicacies: sausages, crackers, preserved vegetables and fruits.

Here, again, another coincidence: Euge and I both have brothers fascinated by cookery.

Rhulera's other business involved making and mass marketing fabric based kitchen items: aprons, towels, table cloths, oven mitts and curtains. She had two lines: one was inexpensive, geared toward the starting up household. The other, which used finer materials, and featured exquisite embroidery on the aprons, and the tablecloths, was geared toward the higher income, or as she said more established, household. She enjoyed designing and cutting out these pieces, putting them together on her machine, stitching parts by hand, especially the embroidery. But had a small crew, headed by her neighbor, Kit, to do that work when she didn't have the time. In addition, this crew delivered supplies, picked up the finished goods, transported them to stores and distribution centers.

When Euge's ankle healed, he returned to football practice, serious horse riding and whispering (which by now totally replaced his earlier, harsh methods of horse breaking). Rhulera and I sewed together and grew increasingly close. We started off sitting on her large, wrap around porch, or in her sewing room, making aprons. We worked quickly together, and mutually inspired creative suggestions. I learned about embroidery, fabric cutting, simple sewing. But as much as Rhulera enjoyed sewing, she had no interest in making clothes. She wouldn't consider putting together a dress for me, a shirt for her, pajamas for Euge; she'd happily buy them. Her favorite things to sew were goods that spiff up a kitchen: cloths, hot pads, window treatments, items that are used and seen a lot. And are immensely profitable. Still, when I confided my interest in making a line of clothing that would include comfortable separates like day skirts, shorts and swimsuits, she, who was remarkably kind but also keen on spotting potential profits, was patiently, incredibly, helpful. Mass marketing, I learned, was Rhulera's fascination; I picked up tremendous business knowledge from her.

■

Our first year away from home, dad, Nantor and I visited my brother who went to college just outside a large dirty—highly entertaining—city for winter break. Selmon, in a newly formed experimental rock band, showed us a tattoo he got on his left leg. Because of his involvement in the band, he was enrolled in only two classes; our family spent long evenings in music venues, listening to his band, and bands of his friends.

The next time we were all physically together was for our spring break; happily Selmon's and mine coincided. We both asked permission to stay at our schools, rather than come home for the summer. I wanted to stay by Euge, and learn more marketing strategies from his mother; Selmon hoped to enroll with his bandmates in a special summer term of camping/music study in the woods. The conversation started after the four of us had a long swim in our pool, and were sitting around, wearing warm up suits made by Nantor. Dad and Nantor looked at one another before presenting Selmon and me with their own, surprising—to us—summer plans.

They explained: when Selmon and I left for college, together, they felt a blank, a void; they experienced *crisis*. Their response: involvement in various forms of physical and spiritual healing, a commitment which helped them decide to spend the summer, and possibly fall and winter, on a quest, which required that they temporarily knock off communication with anyone "out there in the world," even us their children. But they would not do this, would not even consider doing this, without complete blessings from Selmon and me.

I said my father had been debilitated emotionally by losing mom. For years he went through motions: wake up, swim, shower, eat, hug and kiss my brother and me, travel to work, come home, swim, eat, help us with homework . . . but he was always thinking of, or looking at, something else.

He dealt with his grief privately.

He was physically present, though, giving us what he could, and clearly did not want physical separation from my brother and me. He did not want to travel, or stay away over night. That's why the year we both left was emotionally up heaving for him.

This evening, dad started to talk. Saying he'd never healed from losing mom because he just kept stepping forward, that stepping forward helped for a period of time, but wasn't working any longer.

Nantor said a few words herself. That she left behind things in her own past, memories just now creeping back to haunt her. And she feels she can face those things by embarking with dad on this quest.

Ultimately, they hope we as a family, unlikely to be together geographically again anytime soon, could learn to be with one another in our hearts and our minds, if not physical bodies.

I returned early to school—dad and Nantor were pleased

about my boyfriend, and the personal and professional relationship I'd developed with his mother.

I loved then, and truly appreciate now, the body contact Euge and I shared. Our physical relationship was vital: burning and calm at once. Euge understood how to heat up a girl's body; he was also a dead solid sleeper who did not kick and twist, like some others I have slept next to since, do.

Then.

In the middle of my fall term, I learned I was several months pregnant. My period had never been regular, so I didn't pay attention to missing it, and I never felt sick, though my breasts ached. Euge noticed they'd grown in size. When I realized I'd missed a few periods I took a home pregnancy test, on a whim. When it read positive, I was stunned. And when I went to the hospital, and learned I was several months pregnant—with twins—I was shocked.

Two embryos, though, I comforted myself, seemed to *prove* love.

Who, besides Euge, could I tell? Dad and Nantor were off on their spiritual journey; my brother, ill and worn out from recently acquired food allergies was taking time off from school to learn about cooking; I didn't want to divert or upset him (my brother—I thought then—was easily upset and diverted). I adored Bry but did not want to appear needy to her, my MC student (even though she *was* my Big Sister).

Who I did tell was Rhulera. She took my two hands in her own, looked me in the eyes, and asked me to move in.

SEAMSTRESS

At that time, life in the small town still seemed clear, comfortable in contrast to the busy cities I'd spent my childhood in. Sitting on the porch, or in the sitting room with a view, designing, cutting, sewing with Rhulera held concrete appeal. Doing anything with Rhulera held appeal. With her support, I didn't mind telling Bry about the twins, who responded with characteristic kindness and practicality by sharing textbooks and articles from her early Child Development classes on pregnancy. These books were filled with information about weight gain, foods to avoid, fitness during, child psychology, new mothering, birthing, nursing, post partum depression.

I haven't said anything about Rhulera's husband, Euge's father, and it is because I don't trust myself to do so now, because he looks and acts exactly like the mayor.

Rhulera's presentation, unlike most citizens in her small, western town, was more made up than scrubbed clean. She told me from the day she moved there, she was determined to save the town from dreariness, so wore flowing silky gowns, even to water the plants in her flower and vegetable gardens (not, though, to dig in them; she bought pedal pushers for that).

Rhulera and I got into a routine of enjoyable, non-stop work. We made multiple aprons, towels, tablecloths, and started—as I said, at my request—an interesting line of clothing: jumpers and skirts and blouses, giving a twist on homespun type apparel: slim fitting slit skirts; pedal pushers, apron dresses, all in red checks. Things sold well—Rhulera had accurately figured out the consumers to target—and the work was immensely satisfying. Euge continued in school, and helping his dad with the horses. Large, pregnant, I worked, took walks and was sensible with food and diet. I dropped out of school; too embarrassing, too physically uncomfortable sitting through lectures, with my diminishing bladder. And, because of my work with Rhulera I was gaining in something besides size: independence. The clothes I was making with Rhulera earned a good income. She counseled me carefully when the fat checks came in, handing me my portion, one half, of our money, with instructions: "These earnings are yours. Keep them private and safe; they belong to you."

She talked about women and money. Rhulera knew women whose husbands were stingy, and women whose husbands were generous, like her own. She knew women who were born wealthy, and those who worked to get that way like her neighbor who runs the grocery store. The grocery store owner isn't married, Rhulera points out, adding that she believes there is something to this: some husbands would feel diminished by wives who earned more than they did.

My tastes changed. I went from desiring Euge, to tolerating him, to being repulsed by him. By seven months pregnant, he made me physically ill. On the other end of the spectrum, I increasingly adored Rhulera and Bry. Then (swinging the pendulum back) I started detesting the town's landscape, and immense food portions.

SEAMSTRESS

Thanks to Bry I had a relatively easy natural labor: no cutting or stitching. That was good. Here is what was bad: I'm ashamed to say this, but I will: At first I felt nothing for those babies. Red, squirming, causing me nothing but pain, needing attention I couldn't possibly give. Pulling at my breasts (Bry and Rhulera both insisted I breast feed and I did; that pain rivaled labor) leaving them scabbed and bloody. The babies were born in Feb. I didn't feel I could burden my brother with the knowledge (this turned out to be a crucial mistake). Dad and Nantor were sailing on their spiritual journey until next fall. Rhulera helped me, Bry helped me.

I was terrified of my children, couldn't stand their father, adored their grandmother.

When tragic events strike, they really do structure your life. In June, a drunken teenager (driving his family truck) killed Rhulera while she rode her bike down an open road. Now, here I should step slowly and detail, but won't. I can't. I must speed through, skip details. Rhulera's death devastated me. I'm sure it replayed elements of my own mother's death, but it wasn't just that. I truly loved Rhulera. It was Bry who helped Euge and me cope with our loss and our children. And I saw something happening, at first with jealousy but gradually with acceptance and finally relief. It was a developing tenderness—too great to harness—between Euge and Bry. I also saw how naturally and lovingly Bry treated our babies.

Life in that town without Rhulera was inconceivable.

I easily imagined Bry and Euge living together here, together parenting these children; I imagined them encouraging standing, crawling, first words; imagined them covering up tired, chilly bodies, buying seasonal clothes, soothing toddler tears.

I could not imagine myself providing any of this. I was looking into a bleak, black funnel.

In August, when the babies were 6 months, I stopped breast-feeding and switched them to formula. In September I wrote a note to Bry and Euge, kissed my babies and left.

I can't remember my note. I know it included some expression of my relief at their affection for one another and parental abilities in the face of my personal disintegration. I know I begged them to understand and to take care of the children and not to try to find me. I emphasize my state of mind: looking into a bleak funnel.

I didn't include my address (though I sent it later) but knew Bry had dad and Nantor's address, if she ever needed to find me. In fact, Bry and I keep in touch. I haven't seen my children in real life, but she sends me pictures. Smiling babies, perched on Euge and Bry's hips; toddlers riding bicycles with training wheels, wearing Halloween costumes, youths dressed up for junior high school dances, on stage with their junior high school drama club, the two of them, horse back riding.

I don't want to detail more of this right now. But want to say: I do continue what I do for them, and for Rhulera; I carry them all with me.

I did not tell my family about these children. I never felt I was keeping secrets from them, I believed I was closing a chapter of my life, while sparing them anxiety.

I might have told that tale of my past (the children, the father, grandmother and stepmother) unemotionally, indeed, leaving had been a frighteningly easy decision. I could tell you about the sleepless nights, or intermittent bouts of self-punishing behavior I've had since then, but I'm not up to detailing those periods. I'm documenting portions of my history, not all my accompanying emotions. That may be a future project. Certainly those emotions emerge in other areas I may or may not be aware of.

PHYSH

A few days after I stew the chicken, I visit the Pumper. She's anxious about what to wear to the mayor's next party. I listen, thinking how clothing choice is a problem I do not have. Everything I wear belonged to my family, or would have belonged to them. If I am ever invited to a party at the mayor's, I'll wear something like what I have on now: dad's shirt, my brother's belt, mom's tights and shoes, grandma's earrings. The Pumper has so many more options. She views her clothes as old, worn, outdated, when in fact they are classically stylish. Still, she tells me she wants a new wardrobe, adding that the mayor's partner knows a lot about clothes and might be able to help her. I think: The Seamstress could help, then stop. This kind of matchmaking has caused problems for me in the past; I must learn more about the Seamstress and her business before I mention her to the Pumper.

After stewing that chicken, I bake a ham. Trying to learn more about the Seamstress, I follow her beautiful assistant into a grocery store. Once there I lose him—it's a gigantic grocery store—but buy a ham. I carry it to DR's sister's, rinse it in her sink, dry it with paper towel, leave it for two hours while I go to the gym. When I return and see the ham sitting in the sink, I realize it's gigantic and that DR and I won't finish it, even if we share some with his sister's dog. Still, I line a roasting pan with heavy oven foil, bake the ham, decide I can take what we don't eat out to the Pumper—maybe she can use it as hors d'oeuvres for the mayor's next cocktail party. But neither DR or I eat any because of an altercation. Usually I do our laundry. But that morning, DR does it. This change in routine is upsetting enough, but he washes, then dries, a shirt I had stained of my sister's, setting the stain in. Now she's gone and the shirt's stained; I'm not mad, but deeply upset. DR's upset too; we don't eat any ham.

The next day I drive the entire ham out to the Pumper's. I notice that she and DR's sister have identical framed samplers mounted above their bathrooms' light switch. Embroidered in each framed sampler are dogs: Dalmatians, collies, and beagles.

I give the Pumper the ham, and share my suggestion about her using it in hors d'oeuvres for the mayor's upcoming cocktail party. She says, Thanks, but the mayor is entertaining a group of strict vegetarians, who wouldn't want ham at the party. Still, she'll eat some, and so will her neighbors. And we can bring the rest to Happy Hour.

The Pumper and I go to Happy Hour, most people there —the bartender included—are glad we've brought ham. We don't see the mayor, since he's out of town on global business until tomorrow, the day of his party. We sit in a corner, smoke. The Pumper talks about that college boyfriend: his lace-up boots, his natural toothpaste, his unnatural breathing. She tells me how he tells her he's going to an urban graduate school on an accelerated program and that he hopes she'll come with him. He explains that he got a full scholarship, so they can save the money his aunt left him for tuition. He suggests they ask Trowt, ready for a break from city, and to spend real time with his books, to housesit.

For a few months, the Pumper goes with the boyfriend to graduate school, Trowt housesits.

The Pumper and her boyfriend invest the money his aunt left him for tuition, live in a small, on-campus, apartment. She works different odd jobs, wears the clothes she had back when they lived next to Trowt in the city. The boyfriend dresses in his rural uniform: long sleeved overalls, hat with earflaps, lace-up boots.

Trowt turns out to be a diligent letter writer. His letters discuss gardens: planning, planting, but mostly protecting, them. He details his problems with, and solutions for, pests. He builds a three foot high chicken wire fence, to protect against burrowing creatures like rabbits, and—for extra protection—digs a trench and lines *it* with chicken wire. He erects several scarecrows, and strews inflatable snakes—also rabbit inhibitors—throughout his gardens. He is allergic to cats and dogs, but keeps those belonging to the Pumper and her boyfriend, for pest protection. Because of his allergies, he can't keep them in the house, but turns the boyfriend's self-made camp at the property's edge into an animal home. He makes them special meals out of fish oils (for the cats) and bonemeal (for the dogs).

His letters also discuss soil. How he buys a soil testing kit from his favorite garden store in the city, whose results tell him when to fertilize. How he composts anything that was once alive, unconnected with animals. How he turns his compost with a pitchfork, how he sifts it. His letters detail his interest in plant preservation. How he hikes around their land, collects plant specimens then preserves them at home. These activities relax him, without using up the imaginative energy he needs for cooking. Or this is what he writes in his letters.

The Pumper learns more about soil at the end of the school term when she and her newly degreed boyfriend return to the country. This starts their separation. His degree brings him plentiful and lucrative work (the work itself: facilitating interpersonal workshops) which requires frequent travel. He keeps his home base at their home in the country. Trowt continues to divide his time between this home and the city.

A waitress interrupts the Pumper, offers us free beer as thanks for the ham, a more than welcome change from the lunch of boiled eggs, pretzels and dates the bar's owner usually provides for the help. We say, *Yes, more beer.* After the waitress brings us more beer, I tell the Pumper that I think DR's sister could compost in her city apartment; wouldn't compost be excellent nourishment for her balcony foliage? The Pumper agrees. Then we discuss the waitress: her skimpy, boyish clothes and figure, then what the Pumper will wear to the mayor's cocktail party tomorrow night. A man sits in the corner drinking shots of clear alcohol, wearing shorts. That's the celebrated sweater storeowner, says the Pumper, nodding to him. He isn't dressed in a sweater but a simple gray sweatshirt. As we leave, the Pumper points out features in the bar, including the thick logs that make up its walls, and a carved set of initials, hers and Trowt's.

I spend the next few weeks concentrating on my new job, and trying to learn what I can about the Seamstress. I see her crew, but not her. I watch her crew through DR's sister's telescopes, and start to identify certain individual staff behaviors: who laughs, who pays, who walks in front. But I can't learn how they dress since outside they all wear the same ankle length belted coat. I can see them through my telescope, but they blur; I can't see figures individually. I decide I'll walk over, observe her operation, learn what I can about the components individually.

One late afternoon, freshly up and showered from a nap, in a bold mood which I believe was generated from energy sent to me by my brother and sister while I was sleeping, I decide to observe the Seamstress operation. I walk across the street, enter the Seamstress' building. The doorman remembers me, thanks me for not bringing that dog, and asks do I want to see pictures from his vacation. I say, Yes. At that same moment an overwrought tenant bursts in, tells the doorman she's lost her key, *again*. He tells me we can view the pictures later, calls the Seamstress and announces: The pet/house sitter from across the street is here. I'm buzzed up at once.

The elevator door opens, I hear fighting. I don't see the Seamstress or her beautiful assistant, but a woman kneeling on the floor, cutting out material, two big men stand over her say, faster, *faster*, go, *go*, then break up with laughter. What seemed like fighting was humor. I look around. Everything is completely unfamiliar. When I tried to watch this group inside the building through DR's sister's telescope, they blurred. Now I see them individually. They all wear versions of a uniform, creamy, baggy sweat suits. A woman is hunched over a computer. Over her shoulder I see pictures of men's underpants and boxers. She explains they are working on a trouser line, and have to decide what will work best underneath ... besides no underwear, the assistant's choice. He thinks wearing no underwear makes men appear thinner. I study the Seamstress' employees, could they clothe the Pumper? Our materials are expensive, the kneeling cutter says, as if reading my thinking.

No one speaks, but the room is noisy: clipping, tapping, and slurping.

Something about this seems so family. DR and I have a bond cementing us and it is losing families. Our responses

SIMPLY SEPARATE PEOPLE

are in many ways similar: exaggeration of family's importance, admiration for the tight knit groups we feel we can never be a part of, attraction to things temporary. We understand everything is temporary. We really understand this. We attribute our weak and our strong points to our loss.

I want to leave. But don't know how. Everyone continues what they're doing, except for the cutter who stands up with her cut out material, puts it and the scissors on a rectangular table. The assistant, looking stunningly beautiful, walks in, nods to the employees, approaches me, asks where's my dog, and would I go with him to a party for several of his favorite illustrators. If we go early, stand outside, we might catch one of the illustrators pre-party. I think, then say, OK. He walks to and opens a closet, puts on his coat—the ankle length black trench the Seamstress and her entire crew wear, hands me one, explains that rain is expected.

We, in identical coats, walk out the building, smile at the doorman, stand on a curb, the assistant yells, TAXI! On the ride, it starts to rain. I ask, Where's the Seamstress. He tells me what I somewhere probably already knew: She is out in the country working on her new project: founding a dynamic community in an isolated rural region, hoping to bring life and prosperity there.

The Pumper is always like, "The mayor and the Seamstress, this, the mayor and the Seamstress that." Now I understand: we share this Seamstress.

I say, The complex she is constructing with the mayor.

PHYSH

The assistant nods and says, Yes, yes, visibly pleased at what I know.

When we reach the party building, the assistant shows me how these coats transform into rain protection by unvelcroing the back neck of the coat and pulling out a concealed hood. Heads protected by hoods, we stand outside the building in driving rain, hoping to catch at least one famous illustrator. People stream past us into the party. Finally the assistant shrugs his shoulders, says he hasn't seen any illustrators, suggests we enter the party. We do. Pull off our hoods; shake off our dripping coats. My forehead and ears are wet; the assistant, already accustomed to this type of hood-protection, has kept his hair dry, even maintained its puffed style. He rubs his tiny hands together, scans the room. Smiles, points a little finger to a man with a shock of white hair, and weather beaten face wearing a many-pocketed vest, says HE might be an illustrator. The assistant tells me he might have once visited this illustrator, years ago, with the Seamstress. He remembers a person bent over a long table, drawing, in a chilly, windowless room. The Seamstress would not take off her coat. You know, said the assistant, pointing to our discarded, wet ones. It was black, and belted, like those.

I don't know why the assistant takes me to this party but am 100 percent thrilled that he does.

The assistant meets a friend, a choreographer, with very jagged features. He tells us that the man we think might be the illustrator is. And that that illustrator is going to another party. Would we want to go too? We put on our coats, climb in a taxi, the assistant leans back, closes his eyes. The choreographer and I discuss gardening. This starts when I ask him about his foliage-patterned scarf. He says the scarf patterns—burnished leaves, sticks and branches, evergreens—reproduce elements of his lawn in late fall. He asks if I know about gardening. I explain a little about my responsibilities at DR's sister's; grooming her grounds, her indoor and balcony foliage. He asks if my employer composts, adding that even those living in urban environments can compost. I tell him I *had* that idea, but didn't know if it was solid enough to share with my employer. He pulls several fliers out of his suit coat pocket—APARTMENT COMPOSTING—blazoned across the recycled paper's edges, says I can call any time. I put the papers in my purse, planning to read and retain enough to make a well-reasoned recommendation during my next telephone conversation with DR's sister.

I look over at the assistant, still in his leaned back, closed eye position. Traffic is thick; our cab moves very slowly. I want to get out and walk home. We are now actually close to DR's sister's. The choreographer says, Now we're just two blocks from where we're going for cocktails and dinner. Knowing I'll be so close to home, I feel less pressure to get out and go there. The cab lets us out in front of the same building I pass every day with DR's sister's dog during her late morning walk. I tell this to the choreographer, adding that I never knew the building was a restaurant. He answers that it isn't a restaurant, but a club. We walk into the club.

PHYSH

There's the crowd-surrounded illustrator who is talking, smoking, drinking and wearing a foliage-patterned vest similar to the choreographer's scarf. His feet are firmly planted. The choreographer disappears in the crowd.

I want to leave. I miss DR, and have to walk the dog. But there are problems: I have a trench coat not belonging to me; I do not want to disappear and offend the assistant; I never got any information about clothing for the Pumper. I then immediately remember that she has closer access to the Seamstress than I do, should she want Trowt's clothes altered; this is one obligation I can guilt-free knock off my list. I am surprised at how unsurprised I am at who the Seamstress turns out to be.

Deciding that I cannot leave, I head into the kitchen for a glass of water. On my way, I push open an ajar door, see a room whose walls are covered with sunny bright paintings of docks and parking lots. On the floor, in a special bed, sleeps a tiny puppy. I close the door, remembering I've seen that puppy-bed in advertisements, and that the Seamstress designs it. I continue to the kitchen, hoping to find the assistant to tell him about the Seamstress's puppy-bed, and my departure, and in fact bump into him. Before I can talk, the puppy scampers into the hall; the illustrator appears, scoops the puppy in his arms, explains she's easily over stimulated, asks the assistant if he remembers the puppy-bed as one of his employer's designs? The assistant nods. Soon, we are all deep in dog conversation. The assistant tells me that the Seamstress had a dog until a few years ago when a speeding car killed her. The three of us sit silent, very sad. I remember seeing the Seamstress walk alone in the park, wonder if the Seamstress's dog ever played with DR's sister's dog. The illustrator says he'd like some rum. I stand up to get it, ask the assistant would he like something? He stares at me embarrassingly hard, I start turning red. Walking to the kitchen, asking the bartender for rum, I stay red. The bartender asks me why I am so red. I smile, carry the drink back to the illustrator, now the room is filled with people, all talking about dogs. I squeeze the assistant's hand, explain I have to go home.

He says he understands, and to keep the trench coat, compliments of himself, the Seamstress and their crew.

After that adventure, I am very over stimulated, so stay close to my routine. And decide I can learn more about the Seamstress, her employees, and their clothes by looking through my employer's telescopes, and visiting the Pumper, than by actual face to face interaction.

Soon after I walk by a restaurant, see the Seamstress and her crew sitting at the front table. An opportunity for me to enter, say Hello, ask about their designs and prices. But I have DR's sister's dog and worry that might sadden her. In addition, I worry about my new piece of jewelry. I wear the stained shirt of my sister's (I caused the original stain, DR set it in permanently with his wash and dry) and a brooch, an "I'm Sorry present from DR," which covers the soiled area exactly. I am nervous wearing it—it hadn't belonged to anyone in my family—yet this new addition to my wardrobe is what allows me to wear my sister's shirt. Because the brooch is so beautiful, I expect one of the fashion conscious members of the Seamstress's crew, maybe her herself, would ask me about it, which would set up a kind of interaction I hope to avoid.

■

The next time I visit the Pumper, she's sifting her compost with a large rectangle. I wear a hat that different family women—my grandma, my mom, and my aunts—wore. Most people DR and I know go out hatless. But I have an inherited hat and pin collection. The Pumper compliments my hat, but doesn't ask to borrow it. She tells me she needs new clothes to wear for all of the parties that her mayor is giving, adding that if she were larger she could wear Trowt's. Then starts describing pieces of the phenomenally fashionable wardrobe Trowt left here, and some of his books. Would I like to see? My answer is something like, For a rural region, people here sure are into fashion. She laughs; saying it is in large part due to the Seamstress, mayor and sweater store owner.

This gives me the opening I need to tell her how her Seamstress and mine are one and the same.

She laughs, open-mouthed and says, Small World. She puts down the screen and unsifted compost, removes her gloves, and shakes the bandanna off her hair, takes my hand (our first extended physical contact). Leads me inside, up the stairs—the ceiling is very low—down a skinny hall to the library. The room radiates safety. There is a smell here that is fine, and it isn't just from the old books. The Pumper presses a wall button—an entire bookshelf swings open, exposing what looks like a man's shoe and clothing store. Hanging pressed suits, stacks of folded shirts, rows of shoes. Ties, hats and ascots hang neatly from hooks. Who takes such good care of all this, I ask? Trowt did, I do, answers the Pumper, brushing a hanging topcoat. I feel dizzy. Dizzy, deeply falling for Trowt. The Pumper continues: After learning of his oat allergy, Trowt studied cooking and restaurant management. There he learned to vary his techniques: quick tableside sautés, lengthy oven roasts. And to vary the audio component of a dining experience: silence, pumped in and live music. On his visits to the Pumper and her boyfriend, he experimented. The Pumper loved the mini feasts since meals with the boyfriend meant grains, vegetable, minimal oil. And if there was oil, olive or canola. He was totally anti-butter. The boyfriend didn't like electricity, so much of their food was raw, or boiled over a campfire. He bathed using a pump outside, except for in winter, when it was too cold. Then he'd shower inside, using a two-minute timer. When he was away, Trowt experimented with one of his personally favorite recipes: pulled pork barbecue.

I'm reminded of a lecture that I heard last year about pulled pork barbecue. I can't remember many details, because on that day I had a bad itch from what turned out to be an allergic reaction to a new total body cream I picked from a basket of free samples offered at our gym. Which may explain why I remembered the speaker's description of dry rub: massaging a blend of powdered seasonings into a fatty cut of meat before cooking. But when the Pumper went on to describe Trowt's pulled pork experiments (pick a fatty cut of meat which will stay warm while cooking; give it a dry rub; wrap in plastic; roast the meat in a foil wrapping; put it in a double brown grocery bag after cooking), some of it sounded familiar; I had forgotten details.

She goes on to point out to me that the day long process doesn't require constant attention. So while he prepared this pulled pork dish, Trowt read his fiction, and non-fiction books, studied recipes.

On sunny days, Trowt took a special, lightweight and portable chair—it had pockets and also folded up so you can carry it like a shoulder bag—outside with a few volumes of books. Cookbooks, novels, historical fact and fiction. On cold or rainy days he'd stay in the library. At first he kept most of his clothes in the city. But he increasingly yearned for the country, and carted, little by little, his wardrobe out to the home of the Pumper and her boyfriend. All of his furniture and cookware stayed in town.

Looking at Trowt's clothes, I understand what the Pumper says about his large size. Height, not weight. At the other extreme, she is so tiny. Still, I suggested taking one of his suits to the Seamstress, our Seamstress here in the country, or even her crew working across from me in the city, for alteration. She likes the idea, and will ask the Seamstress for suggestions during that evening's menu-planning meeting. I say I did not know she helped with the mayor and Seamstress' menu planning, and ask if her participation is another one of her ongoing tributes to Trowt. She nods, blinks as if keeping back tears.

Back home, DR and I get a fax from his sister, telling us the Seamstress' assistant will stop by this evening, to pick out some tree and bush trimmings for his seasonal hats. I look at DR, who tells me something new: his sister, even now, off on global business, has her clothes made by the Seamstress and her crew. So, I say to him, She doesn't just rely on us for report? He looks at me blankly—his strategy for sidestepping facts he thinks he can't face.

Please walk the dog, I am off to the gym, then grocery store, I say, upset. I go to DR's sister's room, undress, put on a T-shirt that belonged to my brother, rolled up boxer shorts that had been dad's. I'm shivering. Not because of weather. Because I'm frightened DR's sister might consider my reports to her inadequate. Because if she has people: The Seamstress, her assistant, the crew, to fact check against, she might find what I tell her inadequate. Do they know how much I ask DR to do? How often I drive out to the country, the miles I pile up using her utility vehicle? Does she know I went to that party with the assistant? I am growing incredibly nervous. Gym workouts and grocery-store trips often calm my nervousness. But nervousness has turned extreme. When I come back into the living room, DR and the dog haven't left. DR tells me my face looks very blotchy, and that they, he and the dog, will walk me to our gym. Some of the nervousness leaves me. We walk through the park, see the Seamstress wandering down a side path. I'm surprised to see her in the city, and wonder about her menu-planning meeting. DR and I give one another a long look, make a turn so she won't see us or—more importantly—the dog; DR knows the details of her dog loss.

Outside the gym DR pats my back, the dog licks my knees, they head into the park, I to the versa climber.

I'd never tried the versa climber, but had heard it is efficient and effective. After 15 minutes I am deeply sweating, considerably calmed, and ready for the treadmill, the grocery store, the assistant coming to my temporary home. When I finally get there, carrying groceries—mostly dog food—DR tells me the assistant left a message he had a very bad cold, and would come by tomorrow.

The next morning, I wake up with a slight cold. Still I have enough energy to suggest to DR that he and I organize his sister's filing. One of my responsibilities to his sister in this job is filing her mail, messages and faxes alphabetically. While I have been a careful cleaner, plant and tree trimmer and dog walker, I have not been carefully filing alphabetically. Instead, I take the material and put it in a very large drawer, and leave it there, unalphabetically arranged.

I have a problem with alphabetical arrangement. It isn't something that comes easily to me. In that area, I have little detail orientation. DR says he will file alphabetically; I should rest. This makes me upset. This suggestion from DR, that I am incapable of correct alphabetic filing. We work together for awhile, then fall asleep. The next morning I wake up with a very bad cold. Which exhilarates me, though it takes much of my energy. DR, who doesn't have a cold, just a sore throat and ears, brings tea into his sister's room where I'm sleeping, kisses my forehead, says we nearly finished all the filing, then leaves and comes back with a TV. The only channel we receive today is sports. I watch, feverish, with the dog lying beside me. I remember these snatches: horses prancing, trotting, loping. Later, muscular teenagers scale an indoor slope landscaped like a mountain. When I wake up, in early evening, DR had turned off the TV and cleared away the teacups. I bolt up, filled with energy, and hope that DR didn't do any laundry. On my way to check, I bend down to sweep up dog food scattered around the dog food bowl. Fill her empty waterbowl. I sneeze, a bell rings. I look at DR's sister's downstairs door monitor, see the assistant—runny nose, holding clipping shears and a basket. I do not want to answer. He stands, unmoving. Rings again. I answer: Come up.

I am wearing a sleeveless, knee length summer nightgown that was mom's, and sports socks that also belonged to her. My nose is red and very runny. I get tissue before I answer the door. I answer the door, the assistant sees my red nose, says that bad weather seems to have given us both colds. The choreographer, too, has a cold. And the illustrator's puppy has one. He says my arms look very muscular. We talk about the gym: our individual workouts, the ones I do with DR, and the ones he does with the Seamstress. I tell him about my friend the Pumper: her need for new clothes, and also, or instead, heavily altered ones. I do not mention Trowt by name, but do tell him she had a friend, much larger than she, who left a closet (I could have said room) of well tailored suit separates and shirts made from fine material, and we wondered, could he and the Seamstress alter them. His reply was enthusiastic: Yes he'd see them. But must also meet her, learn her personality, see how her body compared to the suits' original owner. I nod, feeling excitement and depression. He goes on the roof, collecting seasonal foliage. I finish cleaning the dog food, and do the laundry, which DR hadn't touched.

Then I look at the filing, am amazed at what DR did with it. Every piece in order, all the wrinkles smoothed out, neat letters on the file folder tabs. All, perfectly alphabetical. I sit, feeling sad, happy, and sad. The assistant, back down from the roof, interrupts to say, Bye. I tell him about my admiration for DR's alphabetizing skills, compared to my own deficiencies in that area. The assistant tells me that, years ago, The Seamstress hired a secretary who was deficient in alphabetic filing. And took down telephone message information erroneously. And she had a gas-passing problem. I ask, was she lactose intolerant, but before he can answer a fax comes from DR's sister, DR and the dog walk in, activating the entrance beeper, the phone rings. It is the music store asking would I fill in for two afternoon shifts next week. Glad to be missed I say, Yes, before realizing I, again, have overextended my schedule. How to fit this in with my responsibilities here, at DR's sister's, and whatever I have to do for the Pumper and her new clothes? I chew my finger, the assistant shows DR what he's taken from his sister to decorate his seasonal hats, the dog laps water. The assistant tells us he has to leave to start these hats: he is very busy, and his cold has set him back. He leaves, DR and I lie on the couch, listen to music. The dog climbs up next to us.

The fax from his sister tells us about a drawer in her dining room's china cabinet that held silver. If we looked behind the silver, we would find boxes of special chocolate for us to eat. We should eat it. She just remembered it was there, if it isn't eaten soon it might become dry and chalky. If we don't want it, give it to someone, like the bereaved doorman. We open the drawer, find several boxes. One for us, one for the doorman, says DR. One for the Seamstress, one for her crew, one for the Pumper, I continue. And one for the music store.

I had never seen this kind of chocolate. The wrapping was brown. C-h-o-c-o-l-a-t-e, in yellow letters, was emblazoned across, a diagonal sash. But when I caught the name embedded into the brown wrapper: Trowt, I jumped.

Now I have two concrete reasons—clothing, chocolate—to visit the Pumper.

■

When I drive out to see her, she stands on a ladder, bucket attached to her waist, picking cherries. After awhile she climbs down, shows me her full pan, and retells me the problem she and her boyfriend had when they first moved into the country and robins ate all of their cherries. She also describes ways she, the boyfriend and Trowt, dealt with it. They covered the tree with bird proof netting, which kept birds away, but the boyfriend disliked the tree's pent-in appearance. Then a neighbor told them that predator birds were an effective natural deterrent. But something, maybe pollution in the area, had depleted the predator bird population there. And buying and importing predators was expensive. They planted mulberry trees with the idea the robins would like that fruit better. Which worked. Somewhat. But what helped most was Trowt's flea market purchase of automatic noise-makers whose clangy sounds pretty much kept robins from the area, and people had fun using them. At that time, Trowt was in a cherry period, using them in stuffing, meat sauces and lemon drinks.

The Pumper tells me these cherries she picks today will go into pies for an upcoming mayor-sponsored bakesale. Would I help her pit? She has 2 other buckets, in the kitchen. On the way inside, I notice a 3-inch barrier of coffee grounds circling her house. She explains coffee grounds keep ants away, and ants seem to swarm her kitchen when she cooks cherries. We wash the cherries in her large double sink, then sit down to pit them. She continues about Trowt: he believes principles of a well-stocked kitchen are similar to those of a well-stocked wardrobe, or library. Acquire well made basics: knives, blue jeans, a dictionary. Then build from there. I ask her about the chocolate. Poor Trowt, she answers. Then says it is possible Trowt is hiding because some (jealous chefs?) associated several deaths with his last batch of chocolate. Not deaths from something put into the chocolate, but several people who bought and ate those bars on the same day were attacked and killed by various pets, with no reported aggressive history, turned into wild, rabid killers. I stare at the Pumper, but imagine I see DR's sister's dog transformed into a beast, attacking DR, start to tell her I have to drive home, I might have endangered some friends, then realize the dog is getting her total body groom, nowhere near the chocolate, which DR and I, anyway, never opened. I decide to wait to tell the Pumper about our stash of Trowt's candy. I just stare at her, and think about family.

The Pumper likes buckets. Of cherries, popcorn, chicken. Buckets of food are very family, so is everyone having a specific place to sleep, not necessarily their individual bed. How can she fathom how upsetting I find her buckets, and things I connect to family, unless I tell her about losing mine? I believe I can heal, DR does too; a snapped heart has a complicated rehabilitative path, but there's the potential. The fact I sense I am about to learn about Trowt, after so much thinking of him, makes me nervous. I start talking about my gym, hoping I don't bore the Pumper, who gets so much walking, jumping, and climbing in during her day to day life out here, in the country, she probably isn't interested. But actually she is very interested, positively brightening at the topic, saying that when she lived in the city she spent a lot of time in the gym. Some days it felt like she spent all of her time there. She launched into a discussion of machines, weight and cardiovascular. DR and I use free weights, so I couldn't discuss machines with her, but was happy to talk about the cardiovascular, and to agree about the pleasures of the ski machines (I tell her about DR's sister's), stair and versa climbers, and the stand-by treadmills. Then comes our longest discussion: the mental and physical benefits of yoga. We would like to learn more by studying with a master. The Pumper says the mayor and Seamstress plan on bringing one out for a week retreat.

Changing the subject, she says someday maybe she could meet DR and his sister. The thought of this brings on a panic. For me. I'm in a stage when I want DR all for me, I do not want to share any of DR with anyone, and I certainly do not want to share his sister. So she talks on for awhile until I shift her back to where I know we must go: to Trowt, his chocolates, the animals that, some said, went mad after their owners consumed them.

She said one version of the story:

Trowt had developed a chocolate in his well-equipped kitchen using double boilers, beaters, rubber spatulas. The home made sweet became a hit with dinner guests. Many rallied around him, convincing him to make and package batches to sell in stores specializing in coffees and confections. A designer friend helped make eye-catching wrapping and lettering which the Pumper said I had probably seen.

One week several people in the city died, all attacked by domestic animals—pets with no violence in their history. Most attackers were dogs but there were a few cats, one snake and a bird. Traces of Trowt's chocolates were found in all victims' digestive systems. One personal trainer had traces on her teeth; she had eaten the candy that recently. More recent

SIMPLY SEPARATE PEOPLE

was the restaurant owner who had a small, ½ melted square in his mouth under his tongue.

Around this time was when he disappeared, which made things seem suspicious. Although people who know Trowt know he periodically disappears. So, she says, he might have vanished for other reasons, adding that she does not know or even really care why he's gone. What she does know is that she wants him back.

I'm wondering what this means for me and DR. Knowing the dog is not home, and that if anyone opened the bars it would be me. Also knowing DR wouldn't take one and give it to someone, the person who did that, too, would be me.

While telling this story, she makes a batter for cherry muffins, a version, she explains, of Trowt's recipe for blueberry muffins. She says she used to like licking the bowl when she made batters, but now, with no one knowing if raw egg is safe or not, she does not let herself.

Trowt, she continues, often developed recipes by talking. This may or may not be why he had installed soundproof walls in both the library and the dressing room he built in their home. She knew because he asked her and her boyfriend to test the sound barrier: Trowt sang, played a radio, talked on the telephone, while she and her boyfriend put their ears to the wall. They did not hear anything. The walls were not thick, but he had lined them with some material that meant they were soundproof. I talk about how noisy the city is, and how you think of needing soundproofing in cities more than out here, in country, and ask, Do you miss the city?

She answers, I do. But explains she wouldn't fit well there now. Having gotten so used to living out here with the rose bushes, the mayor, the Seamstress, their estate, the idea Trowt might return.

I wonder if Trowt misses his books and clothes, but ask if he had an engineering background, since the construction of his library and closet seemed intricate: soundproof, moveable wall units, genius use of space. From outside the house, you'd never guess that such roomy rooms as his closet or library would fit inside it. The Pumper answered that Trowt always said he learned a lot from studying pyramids. I ask, Is it difficult for her to live here without Trowt? She answers, Trowt is always here. I look at her, questioningly. He is always here, she says, patting her stomach.

■

Stop, DR says in a loud voice, filling up the small space of my studio apartment, warning I've memorized enough. That if I keep going I'll over-memorize. That we must break from memorization.

We agree, the memorization I do today wouldn't be my one of tomorrow; each replaying of events expresses itself in its own variation because of factors (forgetting, nervousness, events that impact perception). Each replaying of events from memory turns out different. DR suggests that this break has to come because after a certain point things blur, we can't separate them individually.

Holding hands, we each take bottles of spring water, walk

SIMPLY SEPARATE PEOPLE

downstairs to DR's apartment: an entire floor of rooms. We go to his fitness space and exercise. DR has two treadmills, free weights, and a big screen VCR. Today we run several miles. Then DR leads us through yoga sun salutations, and finishing postures. DR studied yoga as a child, and learned to use it during a time he traveled extensively. His sister practices too. When she travels, she relies exclusively on yoga, since it is physical, spiritual, portable, and does not depend on weather.

We both still go to the gym. But for some circumstances, like this, memorizing so hard for example, we like the privacy of indoor exercise. Eating is different. We don't crave privacy there, so walk down the street to an uncrowded place we can sit down, hear music, eat.

Does memorizing help you remember, or cause you to forget?

I've spent a lot of time emphasizing aspects of my life, but have blocked out several others. I just now told you about yoga. Learning and education is another example. Self-education occupies a big part of my day: reading, practicing, exercises. Maybe not so much now that I'm memorizing. But overall, education was important to my family, so it remains especially important to me, though also fraught with sadness. Sad, yet calm, I continue my process of education. Anything else would be complete betrayal of my family, of all they stood and worked for. Things aren't easy. I used to try and see my family at night in my sleep; that made things worse the next day. Both DR and I have grown since losing families. He used to have a stinging tongue, now he controls it. We both understand tragedy. I'm talking here about activities: gym, cooking, dog walking and these people: the Seamstress, her handsome assistant, the illustrator, the Pumper, stories she's told me about Trowt, his family, his chocolates. These interests provide me with a break, a release, from the heavy load of education, and the losses it reminds me of. Breaks: a view, a drink, an anecdote. Without breaks, things can turn unbearable.

DR and I don't blame too many things on losing family. Our grief counselor once connected my fear of the dark to it. But my fear of darkness has been overactive since childhood. In the day, I think fondly of the night: moon, stars, blue-black darkness are all things I find truly beautiful. But when night actually comes, personally, I have problems. Disturbances creep into my mind.

Everything I work hard to corral all day, stampedes out at night.

Certainly I'm leaving things out of this memory, and distorting their importance. It happened with yoga and education already. I verged on leaving those out. There is the porthole window in the Pumper's bedroom for example, identical to one in my own studio apartment. The blanket once used by her boyfriend that for some reason stays in her bedroom corner on the floor. The spyglass I carry with me in my pocket.

Both DR and I agree that along with sadness comes a kind of safety: the worst has happened; tragedy is unlikely to hit us both again so smashingly.

Tragedy didn't harden out hearts, just got us to erect strongholds around it.

When I think of my family, which I do several times daily, on some days several times hourly, it isn't just the long walks, trips or dinners, but details: dad's neck, my brother's athletic socks, mom's clothes, their edge of gaudiness. My sister's long toes, poking out unevenly from orthopedic sandals.

After eating, DR and I walk, look in store windows, agree not to buy anything until the next portion of memorization is finished, walk more to clear our heads. Then utterly exhausted, we go to my studio apartment, fall asleep, wake up at the same time the next morning and start in again.

■

The Pumper opens a container of vanilla cream sandwich cookies, which reminds me of DR. Not because he and I eat them, but because they are comfort food, and what binds DR and me together is comfort: needing it, giving it to one another. Our families are dead (my entire family, he still has that sister); their bodies won't heal, our snapped hearts might. This understanding connects us; we don't confuse our families' dead bodies with our broken hearts. We're sad, not dead. My family stays with me in daily, non-extreme situations, along through my bouts of deep grieving. Now, for example, I sense mom as I ask the Pumper about Trowt, ask her to continue talking about his recipe development. Trowt, the Pumper continues, perfected his recipes by talking them out to kitchen assistants, friends like the Pumper and her boyfriend, before dictating them into his tape recorder. (Her boyfriend's theory: Trowt's over preparation stemmed from a misdiagnosed childhood learning disability.) He had an assistant transcribe the recipes, then file them in a cabinet—his preferred form of organization. Four times a year, in the middle of each season, taking advantage of food's seasonal freshness, he tested these recipes, and separated results into 3 categories: successful in the kitchen-file, possibly successful in his den-file, unsuccessful recipes, shredded by his shredder.

He perfected recipes the same way he listened to music: in private. Well, not exclusively in total privacy; cooking to him was an activity to do alone, or near trusted friends, colleagues, employees. What he never did was perform. Though he had nothing against other cooks cooking on television, making cooking videos, or performing in wall-less, windowed kitchens, a trend popular in many city restaurants. For example, the Pumper continues, some of the celebrity chefs used by her mayor work publicly in a kitchen without walls, and surrounded by windows, allowing outsiders to look through. Though they often just see the chef's cap bobbing above the heads of fans and students lucky enough to get indoor viewing positions.

When the Pumper first met Trowt, she and her boyfriend thought his insistence on specific ingredients signaled a pickiness problem. But, as they both later learned, ingredient insistence is essential for some sorts of cooks. At that time, the Pumper and her boyfriend didn't know professional cooks (my case too; I learned from cooking books and lectures). Trowt used cocoa butter, not vegetable fats like palm or coconut, in his chocolate. He believed in butter: in its functioning as a powerful, delicate flavoring agent only the smallest number of recipes needed a lot of, but unless baking, preferred ghee. For Trowt, there was always a case for some ghee, and/or olive oil even when cooking and eating spa.

After spending some time with them in the country, he became convinced organic ingredients were the best. Organic ingredients, the Pumper continues, drew him to cosmetics. Ingredients and the Pumper. At one point, the Pumper had a series of allergic reactions—puffiness, tears, wheezing—she attributed to store bought cosmetics. So Trowt and her boyfriend collaborated on a line of home made cosmetics, starting with simple basics: salt mixed with baking powder for toothpaste; beet juice added to petroleum jelly for blush and lipstick; egg white masks for dragging out blackheads (though the Pumper was beyond the age when acne was really a problem), heavy dairy cream mixed with peach pulp for moisturizer (this was more along the lines of what her skin then needed). They would have experimented further except the Pumper discovered the allergy wasn't to cosmetics but to a cat. Not cats (she and the boyfriend had several) but to one single cat who belonged to their mayor, a cat who spent many afternoons and evenings visiting the Pumper, often sitting on her lap. Trowt found an herbal remedy for this, which he never disclosed. In the end, the Pumper enjoyed her mayor's cat, allergy free. And never used chemically laden cosmetics again.

Trowt helped the Pumper and her boyfriend with other practical matters. The boyfriend didn't want to rely on shops to fix things, yet it was Trowt who taught him how not to rely on them: how to mend tires by hand with strips of rubber, a pot of glue and a pail of soapy water; how to unfreeze pipes with a blow dryer. How to build an outhouse for the boyfriend to use those times he felt uncomfortable with indoor plumbing, with the technology.

Often the boyfriend came back from his walks, boots soaked, pants muddy, hands lobster red with cold.

The Pumper worried that his long walks cut into his desire for sex. Unless on his walks he engaged in sex, perhaps through extreme and disturbing actions, perhaps even with or around his special tree.

Trowt could put together excellent meals. For example, eggs, chives, that day collected mushrooms, together with a special bottle of wine he might have brought in his backpack. He prepared these kinds of meals around friendly, intimate company. He could not see himself work in an open kitchen, where any passerby could gawk.

Trowt's eating rules: don't sip after each mouthful, don't lick the blade of your knife (not even a butter you've just used to cut a piece of cheese and has its soft, hard to remove remains clinging to it; *that* would be the work of a piece of bread, or a cracker). Among the few things Trowt refused to serve: raw oysters. He believed, said the Pumper, that, because of ocean pollution, raw oysters were impractical. And he did not believe in large portions of meat, uncomfortable clothing, or extended cocktail hours.

The assistant had told me how the Seamstress has had to monitor their employees, and has even used surveillance to monitor conflict at the mayor's complex. Now the Pumper tells me that Trowt did this too, with those who helped him in his kitchen. Trowt, she says, wanted his staff to pay attention to one another. Know one another's habits, sensitivities, likes and dislikes; rules for respecting each other will naturally follow. This was in the kitchen. Out visiting the Pumper and her boyfriend, however, staff-less he expressed different interests. Like concentrating on his book collection: read them, write in them, take notes using index cards he filed away in a box.

My watch alarm beeps. Actually, it's DR's sister's, she's repeatedly suggested I use it, and I'm glad I did. With this alarm set, I can grow absorbed in anything the Pumper does or says, relying on this external control to keep me on time for my responsibilities. I explain to the Pumper I would like to stay, but have to bolt back to my chores. I drive home.

Once home I walk the dog, then walk to get dog food. When DR's sister first gave me a list of what she expected, she said I'd have to travel out of the city to buy the kind of dog food her dog eats. But when we last spoke, she said she has learned they now sell it at her corner grocery. DR, wearing thick-soled rubber shoes, walks with me. We aren't in a hurry so watch other people walking fast, carrying cups, wearing visible tattoos—necks, ankles, waists. Yes, it is fall but some individuals dress skimpily here. Truthfully, most people whose waist and ankles are visible wear heavy hats or gloves or some warmth compensation. Others, of course, are all covered up so you can just see tattoos on faces.

On our way back we run into the (as far as I could see tattoo-free) assistant, carrying what looks like a carpetbag. He explains it is their new line of imitation fur sweaters and jackets, would we like to see? We would. Upstairs, as he lays them out on our clean dining room table, I ask, Where's the illustrator? About to go on a hiking vacation, the assistant tells me. Yesterday, in pouring rain, the assistant helped the illustrator prepare for his hiking vacation: shopped for boots, a parka and a canteen. It is a day hiking trip, he explains. Nights the group will sleep in hotels; a van will transport their belongings. The assistant, together with other members of the Seamstress' crew, will care for the illustrator's puppy. DR asks, Couldn't the van transport you and the puppy too? He is so little to be newly separated from his owner. The assistant explains, not hiding obvious irritation at DR. The trip is only three days, and it is business, illustrating business, masking as recreation, not recreation pure and simple. The doorbell rings. DR answers, returns carrying a package to us from his sister. We open it up, find a basket of wine, salami, oranges. We all start eating and drinking, and I wonder if this is the time to re-mention the Pumper and her questions about tailoring Trowt's clothes, or to suggest a trip out to her place in the country. I mean to say this, but mention Trowt instead. Instead I mention Trowt, ask if anyone has heard of some chef by that name, who made some special chocolate. DR unpeels his orange, the assistant sneezes uncontrollably. I explain I heard the story while getting gas pumped during a day trip to the country by the Pumper who, in fact, is the woman interested in clothing alteration I told him about. I am saying this, thinking about the chocolate bars stocked up at DR's sister's. In fact, starting to panic about them. I look at DR who appears calm, feel irritation he isn't panicked about those bars. While also considering he may feel panicked about them, but doesn't want to let on in front of the handsome assistant. We don't really know him, or the Seamstress. But after the assistant shows us a line of imitation fur sweaters, he asks us multiple questions about Trowt, which I don't follow because I'm thinking: vault. A vault is a place those bars would be safe—and we'd be safe from them—until we learned more about them. When the assistant finally leaves, with his line of imitation fur sweaters, DR demonstrates he is *steps* ahead of me. He not only had the vault idea, but an action plan: Wrapping the bars in aluminum foil, bagging them in heavy duty plastic, zipping them into a waterproof duffel, taking a taxi to the bank where he puts them in the vault he shares with his sister. Then back here to say we should contact his sister.

■

DR taxis home from the bank, says the bars are safely locked up, in a vault he shares with his sister. The bars that we know about anyway; could there be others, under her bed, tucked into a cupboard, a sock drawer? DR tells me I should know, since I'm the one cleaning.

Over dinner (remains of a lamb-joint, fresh taboolih) I put together out of nervousness while DR taxied to and from the vault, he tells me about a conversation he had with the assistant. I've told DR how the Pumper, like his own sister, keeps her house visitor-ready. Clean, stocked with frozen and canned foods, bottles of beers, juices, waters. Fresh sheets and towels in the guest rooms. The Seamstress, on the other hand, the assistant told DR, despises drop in visitors. So goes out of her way to make them feel uncomfortable. Sheets in her guestroom are clean, but stained. She asks the assistant to bring bad breakfasts: dry eggs, soft toast, instant coffee. Yet if a guest is invited, she cares for them quite well. The assistant told DR (once, when he was here gathering balcony foliage) that he's working with the Seamstress on Just-Saying - No, rather than treating people who drop in so badly.

My own sister and I had this habit where I'd blame things on her, with her "OK," even encouragement. She was that fair, and better equipped to stand up against our parents.

The Seamstress is careful with her staff; Trowt was too, from what the Pumper told me. And also the mayor. My parents were careful who they hired to care for their children, and large home.

Cleaning up, I realize that it's the door of a bank vault, hanging from the ceiling DR's sister uses to hang some of her pots from.

After clean-up, we try to contact his sister, but remember

she's taking a trek to spend some down-time with a group who occupies a couple of caves in a mountainside, sleep in cots, and focus on spiritual grounding. We can't contact her there, but have to wait until she returns to cellular and electronic civilization.

Both DR and I learned to put things out of our minds that are unpleasant, at least in the day. At night, we both can't always do that, which is why we try sticking together. But we put the chocolate bars out of our mind for the rest of that day, and both answer Yes, when the assistant asks to meet us down the street at the elegant, but so often uncrowded, bar for cocktails. The illustrator will be there too. DR and I are both very tired; we discuss pros and cons of our three standard remedies for fatigue: nap, exercise, caffeine, then go on to argue about whether to nap (my idea) or pump some caffeine into our systems (his) before we attempt cocktails. But during our discussion we realize we don't have time for a nap, so get there early, sip caffeine. The illustrator enters. Sweeps in wearing a whipped cream turtleneck, tells stories about famous, now long dead, hunting dogs. The assistant sweeps in next, also wearing a whipped cream color but it's a button down. I wear a grass colored shirt-dress of mom's that I hike up by blousing over my brother's belt. DR wears something black. It became so clear to me that the assistant and the illustrator have sturdy senses of themselves they express in their style. I'd lose my personality around someone like the Seamstress or DR's sister; I couldn't work next to them, day by day. Their personalities would completely engulf me. I do fine with other, indirect kinds of communication. The assistant shows us one of the seasonal hats the Seamstress made with attached bunches of lavender. DR's sister has bunches of lavender throughout her apartment's closets because, DR explained once to me, it not only smells good, but keeps moths away. The illustrator orders himself and the assistant another drink, respecting DR's and my choice to nurse our first, talks about his upcoming hiking trip. Again I think of the Pumper, but decide to explore this chocolate bar issue before I mention her. DR and I have to wait for his sister, but we can also look things up in the library, or use his sister's computer, another one of her household appliances we've put off using.

After some chatting and drinks (caffeine for DR and me, still feeling perilously tired; whisky for the illustrator and the assistant), the illustrator invites us back to his office. Just as we all leave the elegant and uncrowded bar, rain pours on all of us. So we enter the illustrator's office (just a block away) sopping. We take off our shoes, he hands us towels, we dry off, step inside.

It isn't an in-home office, but very home-like: plush carpet and chairs, teapots, a refrigerator. Everything is white: floors, walls, desks. DR asks me, in a whisper, Will he really bring the puppy here, to this white space, waiting to be soiled? I shrug, we hear the assistant tell the illustrator that he and the Seamstress' entire crew use one another as models to fit clothes, to style them. He, hair mashed down from the rain, stands there, startlingly handsome. The illustrator looks

SIMPLY SEPARATE PEOPLE

good too, cheeks flushed, eyes bright. But it is DR who radiates on this day; muscular thighs bulging from uncharacteristically tight rayon trousers. The buzzer rings. In walk two of the men who work for the Seamstress. Dressed in body hugging type clothes, revealing lean, muscular frames. The illustrator wants to meet them, since they will help the assistant care for his puppy. But it's DR and I who talk with them first, because of a series of urgent faxes the illustrator must address. As we talk these two reveal their devotion to yoga, their appreciation of the discipline's inner and outer toning, the cleansing, the equalizing, the way it makes practitioners feel like an explorer. And the unpleasant aspects: the berating one can give oneself for a too heavy earlier meal; the sweat; working next to an unwashed, or even washed but heavily perfumed, person, getting splattered by other's sweat. DR and I detail our practice routine; their attention wanders, I ask about their other interests. Sailing, the assistant pipes in. We discuss sailing, as a hobby, as a sport, as another stress reliever.

DR and I wish the illustrator well on his trip, compliment him on his office, wish everyone else luck caring for the puppy, and go home.

Back home, DR's sister calls, having returned from sleeping in caves, and re-admitted herself to cellular and electronic civilization. Her brother and I each get on a telephone, ask her about the chocolate bars she directed us to. Did she know their history of peril? She puts us on hold. DR wears a shirt of rigorous geometric compositions over his tight fitting, shimmering pants. This outfit erases the shadowy, depressive mood I sense coming onto me. She comes back on the line, Don't, she says Believe what you hear. Then continues, did we ever consider someone could be pulling our leg? Making some kind of rollicking joke about the chocolates? DR and I feel foolish and relieved at once; she changes subject: describes the caves. After the retreat, she stayed in a series of large ones, several had been made into bars and restaurants and a hotel.

After hanging up, DR and I smile with relief. Is the Pumper, we wonder, some practical joker? This is a hard call; am I entirely sure I believe her? DR has many special qualities, but not a developed sense of humor. He often misunderstands people's attempts at jokes.

When we lost our families, DR and I united but not with anger. Not even with grief, though maybe it seemed so at first. Anger isn't enough to unite two people, and sadness really isn't either. We united with a sense of hope, of personal restoration.

When DR's sister returns, we will take up the Pumper's invitation to visit the complex developed by her mayor and the Seamstress.

DR and I try not to rely exclusively on documentation to keep events alive, while also working to keep our attention diverted from past tragedy. In order to keep these events alive, and keep diverted from past tragedy I talk to DR, then he writes this document. I talk, he listens, then writes it out. DR believes that talking something, before writing it, out decreases the mistakes in the written document. The mistakes can be made verbally, aurally, and remain undocumented. My first time through things—recipes, a day or evening outfit choice, a historical journal article—is usually fraught with mistakes, my first time through rarely gets it right. DR said this is the case with many people, which is the beauty of computer cut and paste word programs.

■

While both DR and I suffered extreme tragedies, we also have wounds which are self-inflicted.

And dilemmas. After losing families, DR and me both wanted to stake out identities at once respectful to, and separate from, our dead relatives. Sometimes, we agree, we are too constantly focused on family emulation. We want to be true to family principles, while also updating them.

Tragedy redefines landscape. Our vicious loss sculpted new emotional space for DR and I. Tragedy can diminish, also heighten. Neither of us wanted to be united by sadness or anger; we agreed to veer upward. Still, dark half moons remain beneath my eyes no remedy (creams, sleep, tea bags, ice, cucumbers, fasting) will ever erase. The sadness hasn't gone anywhere. We live with it in our hearts, shoulders, toes.

DR and I met at a group meeting for those who have suffered violent loss. We loved our facilitator. She had pitchers of milk and plates of brownies no one ate but every one was glad were there. We went back the next week, and for several weeks after that, until she—a student intern—flew back to her hometown across the country, to finish her degree. There would be a new intern starting up a new series of meetings; DR and I decided to just meet with one another, and that's how things started between us. We've learned to take time with one another, carefully unpeeling layers.

My mom used to worry about what she described as the humiliation of aging. The humiliation of seeing her face and body and posture change in the mirror. Now, though, she won't confront that. But I, dealing with her tragic death, and the rest of my family's, age prematurely. Even if not yet outwardly. My mom used to say that getting older made her want to stay in, rather than go out and have anyone see her gray, her wrinkles, her liver spots, her slouch.

Reading fashion magazines saddened her, still she loved them. But when she grew older, and didn't want anyone looking at her, she felt conflicted, since the point of fashion was looking. But is it unhealthy, she wondered, if you like looking at others when you don't want others looking at you. Except maybe pictures of how you looked in the past.

In the beginning my grief was fragile, dark yet comforting. I didn't want contact outside of it; when outsiders came in (counselors, consoling friends, doctors) they wrecked my suffering, stomped, intruded, with their weighty presences. DR was, and continues to be, different. We were so sad by the loss of our families we refused tears. Discussing this later, we learned we both cried often, and frequently when responding to small irritations.

DR and I refused tears after our losses. But we did grow interested in surmounting the tragedies; in making sense, stories, of the past.

A car, of course, means different things to different people: Do you own one, can you drive one? Have people you love been harmed in one? Depending on your viewpoint cars can be tragic; comic; used for racing, transporting, or showing off.

Memorizing our house sit and things happening during it is a healing exercise. Letting sad things from my past, and DR's, slip in but not dominate.

For a long time I've chewed gum because I read it was good for teeth, and everyone in my family had had weak teeth. For that reason, I never drink carbonated sodas.

PUMPER

Insecurities make some people work harder, while they diminish drives in others.

Those I describe as wanting some sort of "life in the country"—that boyfriend, the mayor and the sweater store-owner—did so for various reasons I connect to their varying levels of personal confidence.

My boyfriend's goal was to get away, to prove something. I am not sure what, and despite the fact I am not sure *he* ever learned what, I believe that he achieved it.

The mayor with his vast experience and many connections, doesn't have to struggle to make a credible image, or his country venture successful. For him, the country holds potential he calls Luxury Organic.

This mayor has a good eye, and a deep appreciation, for

trends. He encourages—but doesn't require—cutting edge dress. Silky pants (both the baggy and stove-pipe fit), body conscious sweaters, kaleidoscopic suits, plaid kilts, are examples of the fashion worn by many of the mayor and Seamstress' guests. At the same time, there are also the more traditional guest outfits such as khakis, t-shirts, boating shoes. Neither style appears out of place.

The sweater store owner, particularly if he's been heavily drinking, gets in moods where he gleefully destroys beauty: pops the flower bud off its stem, smashes his fist, even elbow, into the center of a layered pastry. Being in the country, in its open space, he says, lets him blow off steam, "harmlessly."

He works hard, designing his sweaters, which combine practicality, durability and style: each piece has a lot to offer: protection (from rain, cold), permanency and low key elegance. He started off knitting and putting them together himself. But then became so busy and successful, he hired local workers to construct them. His reputation as a designer and producer is solid: exceptional product; exceptional labor relations. There is a lot to admire about this man, in addition to his abdominal muscles.

I deeply admire physical fitness, especially when it comes with obvious effort. When I run early in the morning, I often run into the sweater store owner running, or I see, through his upstairs window, in street view, his head bob as he rides his stationary bike.

I have an older and younger brother. My older brother and I love—yet have nothing to say to—each other. I hope that be-

PUMPER

cause our affection current runs so strong, our communication improves with age. When we were young, he pulled my braids, made fun of my music, read my diaries. But now I understand this aggressive behavior as some kind of affection display. My younger brother, in contrast, always off in his good-natured world, didn't display that kind of affection. My parents, too, were good-natured. My older brother too, just not especially always to me when we were little. He's now a stock trader, also an avid downhill skier.

My boyfriend was an avid downhill skier, then gave it up because, he said: 1) the expense; 2) a belief that global warming would render the sport obsolete; 3) it was environmentally damaging. But in graduate school he met peers and professors, who downhill skied, so started up again. This morning I get a postcard from him and my older brother, skiing together. When I first read the card, I feel the equal pulls of irritation and relief I wasn't invited to ski that sparkling alpine slope, am instead out here in my home in the country, waiting for Trowt, preparing for our mayor's upcoming party, saving money and collecting information.

I'm always invited to parties at the mayor's, never expected to bring anything. But I learned so much from Trowt about hors d'oeuvres; I always bring them as an (unspoken) tribute to him. My way of keeping Trowt present. And when I cook hors d'oeuvres, I pretend Trowt watches. This makes preparation pleasant. And clean up minimal, since I am especially neat and systematic when I imagine he watches.

I learned about food from Trowt; continuing my educa-

SIMPLY SEPARATE PEOPLE

tion and interest is one small way I pay tribute to him. I learned about clothes from the Seamstress, or am starting to, so try to pay tribute to her by dressing the right way. My cooking skills, so far, exceed my fashion ones.

The Seamstress and the mayor, two of my favorite people, enjoy the foods I make, or say they do. But no one out here has ever highly complimented me on an outfit I selected on my own. Although I got frequent compliments on my work outfits when I lived in the city.

The mayor, Seamstress and I meet once a week for menu-planning, and to eat an informal snack. A pitcher of lemonade and plate of wafer cookies in the warm weather; milk and cream cheese chocolate brownies in cool. I make those cream cheese chocolate brownies. Sometimes in cool weather, the Seamstress makes her special donuts, which are crisp outside, moist in. Lately, the three of us get together for a monthly meal. The Seamstress picks the menu. Last month it was a wild mushroom sauté over rice. The month before that, steak, potatoes, brawny red wine. The mayor, Seamstress and I lean toward vegetarianism but aren't strict.

My boyfriend, who by the time we moved to the country was devoted to strict vegetarianism, loved to say things like: The servant is always a master in disguise.

Which makes sense, I'll admit, in some circumstances, but certainly not all.

Here drips the perspiration.

■

PUMPER

My parents are currently off researching a marine biology project. My younger brother, having chosen that field too, works with them. These three family members share a quality of intense concentration. My brother's girlfriend, researching with them, has that same brand of concentration. She wears short, stylish hair, heavy make up, but you'd never see her in anything that was low cut, or had lace or bows. She looks so much like my younger brother you'd think they were siblings. Which is possible, since he's adopted (all three of us are). We don't know his lineage, I've never asked about hers.

For a few years, my younger brother sat to urinate, which our then next door neighbors said—out of our parents' hearing range—was odd. But that completely stopped.

Maybe I have abilities in science, and they'll reveal themselves in time. For now, and since I can remember, I've excelled in things having to do with physical motion: climbing, swimming, running.

And observing people. Certain people, at certain times.

Researching people is part of why I operate my service station. Everyone who drives out here needs gas; pumping it, I can see who they are, learn their names, even addresses, discover if they have children, which state they are from, their tastes in clothing, music. I also take care of car trouble, auto mechanics being something I've studied and have a—to me surprising—aptitude for.

I left college to earn money waitressing. My family was off spending our savings on a science experiment our government retracted funding for. I was invited on the research trip, located in a set of South Sea islands, but what would I have done? Swam, fished, scuba dived; all activities I could have enjoyed. But those days I was uninterested in enjoyment, veering toward the overly serious (my boyfriend had this tendency too). Still, my emotional organization then was what it was. When I catch myself wishing that I *had* gone, I bear in mind that *that* emotional organization led to the life I lead now, out here in the country. Which, even if it involves waiting for Trowt, I find rewarding.

Am I accurate when I describe my boyfriend and me as overly serious? Maybe. But it's closer to the truth to say we went through periods of being simply no fun. Take a stage of our eating habits.

I'm sweating less as I remember more. Detoxification, or renewal?

When we left college and moved to the city (he graduated), I regained my ability to eat meals anytime any place. That development was good. But from early in our relationship, my boyfriend and I needed enemies. Our enemies changed over time, many never lasted more than a few months. Among the short term enemies: unnatural fabrics; medication; good food. We made sarcastic remarks about people who made a fetish of (our term) good food. We ate unappealing meal combinations. Dinner on a good night meant peanut butter and jelly sandwiches, but usually it was something even less appetizing such as: thin tomato sauce and spaghetti, or even soup (not cream of mushroom) eaten cold and from the can, shoe string potatoes (also from a can), spoonfuls of sweetened cocoa, and of peanut butter, sometimes mixed. Those sorts of combinations. Beverages were powder mixes: I've mentioned cocoa, there was also Kool Aid, chocolate milk, Hi C. For dessert we poured imitation syrup over vanilla or chocolate pudding cups.

Cooking carefully, we rationalized, was self absorbing; shouldn't we spend our time on other, more important things?

That mindset altered soon after we met Trowt, and transformed once we moved to the country.

■

Our city apartment had a large kitchen, but was otherwise small. The kitchen window looked onto a busy, store studded, street of audio, drug, video and shoe shops, and directly faced a popular 24-hour grocer, that "went organic" just weeks before we moved in.

I sat for hours at our kitchen table, watching the organic grocer customers; the activity would keep me sharp for my research job. Because the store's outdoor lighting was bright and far reaching, my watching hours were totally flexible.

Stirred by Trowt, my handsome, food focused, neighbor, I paid careful attention to the bread and greens poking out the tops of customers' bags, and the wide range of drinks they left the store sipping: bottles of water, multicolored blends of squeezed juices, steaming cups of lattes and teas. These looked, from my post, tasty and recreational. When my boyfriend and I finished the last of our Hi C powder mix, we walked over and tried one.

Now, the thing my boyfriend and I had in common with food was, what.

Rebellion.

We both grew up in homes which considered food monumentally important. His mother, a ballerina, cooked everything he ate from scratch, using the oil, grains and dates sent by relatives; meat from the specialty butcher; fresh ingredients from her small fruit orchard and extensive vegetable and herb gardens. And my own parents, distracted as they were by science, children and pets, took cooking seriously. Cooking, eating, these efforts *actualize* science, they'd say.

When my boyfriend and I finished the last of our Hi C powder mix, we walked across the street, purchased and enjoyed specialty drinks (soy cappuccino for me; carrot, beet juice blend for him), we were easily hooked by good tastes, so familiar from our childhoods. We went shopping, were thrilled to buy: a sturdy loaf of bread, complexly flavored cheese, fresh produce, a pear tasting like pear, zucchini like zucchini, lettuce (romaine was our favorite) that tastes. My boyfriend rejected any oil or spicing, preferring bland, dry preparation as a way to honor the food's integrity. I sometimes added vegetable oils and spices to my individual portions.

We had separate personal reasons for favoring careful food selection. My boyfriend's motivation: the political and economic ramifications of supporting stores that sold clean—i.e. not chemically laden—foods.

My motivation: attracting positive Trowt attention.

Trowt's long, varicose veined, legs. Their strategically placed tattoos.

At first, when my boyfriend and I moved out here, to the country, we imagined a village economy. Imagined that we would travel for supplies. But with the mayor and his guests building up the town, specialty items are everywhere.

Here's a thing about me, and I'm not bragging or idealizing. My family is extraordinary: unpretentious, entertaining, well mannered. We were plugged into a vast, tight, scientific-family network; families whose parents worked together, lived in different parts of the world, relied on one another for support.

My boyfriend said I idealized my family, until he met them. When he did, he retracted that opinion. Said it was understandable that growing up, I never felt like leaving them to seek other company. Kids at school and on the block were fine, but I didn't laugh as hard as I did with mom, dad, my brothers; didn't have to work as hard to win at checkers, didn't have to run as fast to get caught playing tag. As a family, we enjoyed the company of other people, but not as close companions; we used each other for that.

My boyfriend had a dense, tragic family situation. Relating it is a crucial portion of this recounting. I am not up to detailing it now.

SIMPLY SEPARATE PEOPLE

As upsetting as I find his family history, recalling it doesn't make me sweat.

Just thinking of him starts that.

Though, as I just mentioned, decreasingly so.

■

When he asks me about mom, I explain the pets, the pipe, the casual attire, the three solid daily meals. When I ask him about his mom he answers: "Every swan has her song," then sighs in a sarcastic, tension releasing way. (Eventually, he elaborated.)

My scientist parents. Mom had careful manners, for example, would never open up the refrigerator to dig her fork—let alone index finger—into a piece of pie on a plate or in a tin there. Dad, who dressed with a careful elegance, might. But probably wouldn't have if he absolutely knew someone was watching.

My parents were together a long time before they adopted us. I don't think kids were a hard transition, because before kids they had pets. Goldfish and guinea pigs, which may not be complex enough to sustain real relationships, but also cats and dogs; pets whose needs resemble young children's: food and water, toys, hair brushes; walks to the park, trips to the doctor and bathroom. So adopting kids couldn't have been a big transition.

They also studied butterflies, belonging to their then artist neighbors who bred butterflies in an enclosed, butterfly plantation, and earned a portion of their income releasing them at parties (always using native to the region species, so as not to disturb any gene pool). When the butterflies died their (natural) deaths, these artist neighbors put together pleasing collages using the tiny, brightly colored scales of the deceased butterflies' wings.

Much about Physh is very mom and dad. From what I know of her, she's practical. While my boyfriend always talked about the importance of taking a careful approach, Physh, who never talks this way, *behaves* practically. Which is why I wasn't surprised to learn the car she drove belonged to her employer. That jeep, an expensive, popular model, gulps gas, and has immense cargo space she doesn't need (aside from her employer's dog, I never see her transport anything, and the dog could fit into a front or back seat, wouldn't it?).

Yet, unlike my parents, Physh has an energy economy problem, believing at any given moment, she either possesses too much, or too little. In one of our early conversations, she tells me that she has specific troubles with excitement. That it's a kind of energy she can't effectively harness, that it distracts her to the point, nearly, of not being able to function. That when she's excited her attention darts from thing to thing, "like a staccato note," but cannot land anywhere, cannot take root.

Physh, I say, I understand. But only when remembering myself, pre-Trowt. Loss has matured me. Losing my boyfriend, Trowt and life in the city have all increased my energy efficiency. Now, I generally seem to have the amount of energy I need; not more than that, but not less either. Still, when

Physh explains her terrible problems with energy management, it is something I understand. The batch of emotions I've collected for Trowt helps me manage my energy. Her current job—working across the street from the fashion house of the Seamstress, our Seamstress, known for her aesthetically powerful yet easy designs—helps her with energy management.

REMINDER: ask Physh if she knows how much the Seamstress has shifted away from clothes, and towards planning and implementing the mayor's complex.

■

My opinion of Trowt is confused by my impression that his deepset, worried eyes never matched his informal and relaxed behavior.

When my boyfriend and I moved out to the country, he and Trowt united in a common cause: organic gardening and food growing possibilities. While my boyfriend was active in our own land plot, community organizing, night hiking (and, for an extended, marathon training period, night-running), he also helped Trowt scope out wider reaches of the region.

They both operated under the sound assumption that to grow a healthy crop, you work with your land; make it strong, not sick. They were both, at this point, anti-genetically engineering food. Mapping out the soil quality of particular fields, using a tractor mounted computer and global positioning device, they encountered miles of streams and pasture land that were seriously polluted.

PUMPER

They witnessed results of bad farming; our neighbor lost his pumpkin crop because his soil was ruined through chemical treatment, which eliminated all the weeds and worms.

They met wholesalers who only grew iceberg lettuce, and talked these businesses into diversifying by growing varied organic greens (endive, bib lettuce, cabbage). They helped the farmers—many tired and defeated from sick animals and broken machinery—supplement their income by creating Pick-Your-Own berries, apples, flowers sections of their farms. Visitors would stop by, pick and pay (a good activity for families, couples, groups of friends, out in the country wondering what, now, to do), or buy already picked bushels. Of course, once the mayor's parties got started, he and his guests accounted for a large number of customers.

Some would call my attitude toward Trowt idealized. They would say what Trowt and I have is based on something unreal. OK, to some degree my feelings for Trowt are make believe; what love isn't to *some* degree invented. Still, I haven't seen Trowt deal on certain—I'll call them egocentric—levels. My boyfriend, in contrast, craved specific kinds of attention. When I first met him, he wasn't sure which kinds of attention. But college, meditation, living in the country and then graduate school helped him to discern that. Those experiences didn't eliminate his need for attention, but did help him figure out what specific kinds.

I'm not saying anything here I wouldn't say to him; we spent hours discussing this. My boyfriend had a difficult upbringing. I can't use that excuse for my insecurities and

SIMPLY SEPARATE PEOPLE

doubts. It isn't easy, coming from a loving family. A nurturing, stimulating upbringing doesn't always prepare you for the grim realities of our world. I grew up extremely protected, so was unprepared for some of life's realities. Maybe this explains that bizarre eating condition, and my series of odd sexual crushes. One was on a stocky, sunburned boy (I only saw him during summers). During the first few summers I was attracted to how he put his hands in his pockets. One night, a group of us made a campfire, drank some punch. I left the group, squatted peed, wiped myself with a leaf, stood up, pulling up my shorts; a flashlight beamed on me: it was HIM. I laughed; but when he, in return, giving me an expression I can only describe as appalled, bolted, I felt wretched. I adopted his reaction, and felt wretched.

A few years later, I saw that teenager do something unspeakable at a party, well, in a barn behind it. We were at our summer house, I got off my baby-sitting job, and was, as usual, over excited to be heading for a party (remembering this helps me understand Physh; her challenge to tame excitement), I floored the accelerator on my way to a party. I drove recklessly, fast; High Damage Potential. I got to the party flushed and breathless, had some punch, walked outside to the barn, whose open roof gave a star studded night view. Instead of encountering more friends—this makes me sick writing this, it doesn't make me sweat, it makes me sick—there was that sunburned boy sitting spread eagle watching a nest of newly born kittens, slowly stroking his erect, beet red member.

What upset me the most, was that I could have ever felt sexual feelings toward that kind of person.

I couldn't bring myself to relate that story to my boyfriend.

Whenever my boyfriend discusses his mother, I feel I could have been her. A version of her. Had I continued along that track of reckless driving. Instead, I've developed strength, a firm exterior and solid control.

"Anything that touched her was like a knife through a soft thing," my boyfriend said about his mother.

I've learned from the mayor. The mayor started his virtual community complex in response to an alarming observation: people, whether living in the city or out in the country, growing increasingly isolated from what is immediately around them. He, in turn creates a friendly, people centered place with good food, neighboring stores, and entertaining activities. Though I think this would have stayed in the concept stage, had it not been for the Seamstress. The mayor is anti-over consumption. He believes people should own a few, high quality things (pairs of socks, tubes of creams, sets of sheets). My boyfriend, too, was anti-over consumption, yet placed no importance on high quality things. Believing high quality is something inner to cultivate within yourself, not buy, wear or drink. Which sounds so good, and I'm not saying too good to be true.

After my boyfriend left, I taught myself how to seriously cook. When we lived together, I knew how to functionally, not seriously, cook. To learn how to seriously cook, I started with 4 of the basic taste sensations: salty, sweet, sour and bitter. I practiced expressing them in different recipes. From Trowt, I learned to deeply appreciate how fortunate we are out here, in the country, with fresh food. Always remembering not to assume food safety; our own stream was soiled with sewage, but our neighbors' tested pollution free.

I learned how to use beverage to enhance a meal, whether it was plain water, good beer or a mix. Say, crushed ice, a bit of condensed milk and fresh fruit. Or an alcoholic mix: 1 part alcohol, a dash of something sweet and light, a simple garnish. I studied the science of wine. Eventually, I taught myself pastries like the complex napoleon, a neat rectangular stack of contrasting tastes and textures, cut with a fork—not knife—when consuming. Another thing that happened after my boyfriend, but before Trowt, left: I noticed ripples on the backs of my thighs, and berserkly traveling veins all over them. Not varicose, like Trowt's.

This degeneration convinced me it was time to enjoy myself.

My boyfriend's mother's life was cut short, preventing her from fully enjoying herself.

I understand the benefits of enjoyment, also understand it can lead to tears, carelessness, tragedy. For me, the practice of cooking channels enjoyment, lessening—for example—alarm at my rippled thigh backs, and the veins traveling berserkly everywhere on them. Excitement, like any unharnessed form of energy, can lead to danger, such as reckless, desperate driving.

My boyfriend described his mother—who, incidentally, died while driving—as being personally under-protected.

PUMPER

Which may have contributed to her greatness as a ballerina, but did not contribute, he believed, to her abilities as a mother or social person. Things in her behavior, not the dancing, deeply embarrassed him. Her death left a hole, a scalded space. One of the reasons he was attracted to me, he said, was that I helped him to talk, to heal that scalded space. I liked the rhythm of listening to him: regular talk, more talk; then, eruptions of almost unbearable brightness. Then back to regular talk, talk.

When his mother died, his kind and wealthy aunt took care of him. His mother explained to him, she did not know his father, a statement his guardian aunt verified but he himself never 100 percent believed.

■

Years before I met my boyfriend, I knew about his celebrated mother, a ballerina famous for her exquisite dancing, successful film career, ethereal beauty, and tragic early death.

I first saw her in a documentary shown in my fifth grade gym class. In the opening shot she sits, tiny and erect, on a balcony overlooking a raging sea, dark eyes flashing, famously short blond hair moving in the wind, speaking English with a heavy accent; her interview was alternated with clips from dance performances. Two things struck me then: her face, which in addition to being beautiful was expressive, always on the verge of some profound pleasure or deep pain. What also struck me was my impression that this woman has an absolute ballerina speech as well as carriage. Her speech, elegantly lilting and muscular at once, seemed so ... *balle-*

rina. I wasn't sure what that meant then, and am perhaps less sure now, but in fifth grade, watching the documentary, it was my strong impression

The documentary did not mention her son, later to be my boyfriend, who I now figure was age 9 at the time the film was made, six years before his mother's death. When I read in the paper she died in a car accident, I felt someone I was connected to, even deeply admired, died. Yet I hadn't met her. She was killed while driving home late one night; investigators guessed she fell asleep at the wheel (she always drove herself, never trusted anyone's driving skills but her own). There were no traces of drugs or alcohol in her body, no traces of any foul play. But some members of her ballet troupe thought she may have become ill, either from an allergic reaction, or food poisoning, because she had come out of the bathroom not long before she left a post performance party looking queasy. Some (not all) troupe members and party guests who had nibbled at the post-performance buffet catered by a local chef got mildly ill from—it was later discovered—the smoked whitefish dip. Yet no one who knew the ballerina could imagine her ever eating smoked whitefish dip. So, while the likely cause of death was falling asleep at the wheel, nothing was ever proven.

When I met my boyfriend and found out he was not only motherless but who his mother was—someone who fascinated me; someone I loved in some way—I felt instantly linked with him.

Soon after we meet he tells me one recurrent childhood

PUMPER

dream: he and his mother are at a beach. She goes into the water, he suddenly hears her yelling, drowning. Torn between running to get help, or plunging in the water to save her, he is gripped by momentary, frozen, indecision. He decides to swim but when he reaches the water he "remembers" that he cannot swim (in fact, he was and is an exceptional swimmer), he runs to get help but not in time for a rescue. He wakes up from this dream soaked, panicked, frantic at his helplessness.

When his mother dies in the car accident, he feels responsible; the same sort of helpless he experienced in his dream. His favorite aunt, the unmarried sister of his mother, the dean of a highly respected and competitive boarding school, becomes his guardian. He adores this aunt; and believes, even at that young age, he is better off emotionally being raised by her, rather than his, albeit, luminous, world renowned mother.

This is knowledge that made him feel, and still makes him feel, guilty.

He describes his mother as crazy, non-obviously. When I first ask for an example, he shows me this letter she wrote him after he won a prize for elementary school drama club:

My son,

You've accomplished so much at your young age; don't I seem terribly dull by comparison..... Mother

He reads the note aloud, then asks me, tears welling up in his eyes, waving the note in my face: Do you think that she—

SIMPLY SEPARATE PEOPLE

world famous celebrity—wrote this out of some sadistic cruelty or pure dementia?

Dancing was his mother's first passion; gardening her second. She'd converted the guest house behind her home (it overlooked her considerably large and well organized grounds) into a practice space. Within weeks of her death, her closest colleagues and friends turned the space into an homage to her: performance costumes, family photographs, baby pictures, a young girl with her sister and parents, dancing as a child and adult, holding her infant son, giving him his first swimming lesson. The place, which had the feel of a shrine, was also adorned with anecdotal objects: tiny portraits carved on pebbles or painted on miniature medallions. One long antique table was devoted to the presentation of a selection of her personal letters and papers. A friend had made a sort of collage out of lines from her journal: Here is a quote following the explanation of her personal garden which she loved, and kept orderly, not wild:

> My vegetables live in lines, not groups; I love the linear. The neat rows of potatoes and carrots. I cried this morning; those tears watered my zucchini. When I'm reincarnated, I hope it is to a zucchini, I love that very pretty vegetable.

Another passage is from a page on a doomed love affair:

> It's morning again, not morning still, time speeds by at a frightening pace; we never forgive people for aging. Parents, teachers, lovers ... Passion for youth is masochism, not purity.

PUMPER

One of the dancers in her ballet company gave her a plaque:

> I AM LARGER AND BETTER THAN I THOUGHT
> I DID NOT THINK I HAD SO MUCH GOODNESS

Her friends found it in her basement, a signal to them she did not love it, so they decided not to display it.

Portrayed by friends and media alike as intensely passionate, this woman deeply enhanced the lives of the men and women around her. Her last lover, an artist who who kept her shrine, gave her a nickname: Lora, then it became "Laughing Lora" because whenever he saw her in his dreams, or imagined her, it was laughing. His series of drawings, titled, *Lora Laugh and her Giraffe* depict Lora, a figure carrying a dead-on resemblance to the ballerina down to her pinkie ring and neck birthmark, sprawled spread eagle on her back, head and (inventively long) pubic hair blowing wildly in the wind.

The space functioned as a sort of time capsule for my boyfriend; it affected him differently at different times in his life.

Now, just tiny beads of perspiration are dotting my forehead, and upper lip.

■

Sometimes around Trowt I felt divided into two people. Especially lying in bed, listening to the radio station my boyfriend tuned to whale sounds, bluegrass or baseball games, knowing Trowt was just next door, maybe lying down too. But I convinced myself for the longest time that when I slept,

SIMPLY SEPARATE PEOPLE

a part of me stayed there, warm and sleepy, and another part awoke, traveled through the walls to Trowt, returned to wake up next to my boyfriend, his radio station.

A series of logical steps that lead to surprise sums up my take on cooking, Trowt would often say.

He once told me, during a cocktail hour that was very long (he did not cook, a colleague did; Trowt was uncharacteristically lightheaded), that a family friend used to say, tousling his hair, "Put your tongue to good use before it gets ripped out." Which he thinks explains his non-stop work ethic. Not fear of losing his tongue, but his awareness that an event: bolt of lightning, out of control car, terminal illness, could alter life as he now knows it.

Cooking excellent surprises is all that lies between me and something pitiable, Trowt often growled.

When I started seriously cooking, I remembered a lot of things I'd learned listening to, and watching, Trowt. His practical inventions, for example. When blending, he covers his standard mixer with a washcloth to minimize any splatters. When straining broth, he stretches a double layer of pantyhose—or knee highs out of the same nylon material—over a container (bowl, cup, jar). To relieve the gas problem sometimes caused by eating beans, Trowt adds fennel and often a bay leaf. And I've seen him wear a snorkel mask when cutting onions, but I wasn't sure if he seriously used this to prevent tear flow, or if he was comically performing, the way the mayor used to, and still in fact sometimes does.

He also taught me not to feed our cats very much, since

then they'd be full and not eat the mice we hope they get rid of.

■

My family is extraordinary; don't judge them if you aren't impressed by my recounting. This is not their fault.

My parents lacked the self absorption pronounced in so many of their renowned scientist colleagues. I remember a time when our pediatrician praised my mom on the way she and dad raised us, explaining, "Every parent finds their kids amazing. But you and your husband, you two, on the other hand, find *kids* amazing. You two just love kids."

Later I asked mom, would she be more possessive towards us if we were her biological children. Her (characteristically honest) answer was, You know, I'd really like to *think*, no.

Relationships can start off all heat and night and heavy sky; kissing, singing, poetry writing, then something can turn its dank and destructive tap on. My parents' happy marriage is an exception. They have that fascination-with-science bond. And they're devoted parents.

There is a fine line between fascination and over involvement. For a period, Trowt told me he became over involved with food—not that he ever ate it too much, but that he thought about it too much—and wished that he could be like his friend's dog; eat a healthy mix once a day, then move on. Which reminds me of something the Seamstress said about clothes. She, at one point, wished she could go back to approaching them the way she did the year she went to a high school that required a uniform (her stepmother disliked that intensely) recalling—wistfully—days when she thought less about presentation.

My curiosity, if unchecked, definitely extends to over involvement; confining it to a duty—my profession—keeps it in check. At work, I enjoy getting information, asking questions. But I steer away from overtly violent forms of dysfunction: drugs, murder, armed robberies. These subjects frighten me too much to effectively investigate them.

When I first met my boyfriend, leggy, fair haired, he wore oversized white shirts, I guess, similar to the costumes he grew up seeing his mother's male ballet colleagues wear. But he wore them with blue or black jeans, not tights. I keep remembering odd moments from our time together. Like one morning when I walked in the bathroom, surprised to see him taking a bubble bath. He held out a soapy hand, ran it over my cheek.

At this point I'm barely perspiring.

Or once when I drove home from the city, and saw him in pounding rain, standing next to his bike which had a flat. He—a figure standing there in the glare of headlights, waving arms like a huge puppet—had uncharacteristically forgotten his pump. I had mine in the car, but because of the pounding rain we loaded up the bike and drove home to one of our more romantic evenings, this being just after he learned about acceptance to graduate school.

■

PUMPER

While I'm not deeply curious about Trowt, certain questions come to mind. Where for example, did he go? Off to explore himself; to explore the world; was he was kidnapped; did he die of something sudden like a heart attack or injury, in a remote place? Or maybe he participated in a secret scientific experiment, sending someone back in time or out to space. I understand these are all possibilities, I choose to believe he's hiding.

There is the fact he disappeared after his chocolates turned pets of those eating them violent; his absence might be connected to this. If so, I am convinced Trowt will emerge totally guilt free.

Yet, this case, so close to me, isn't one I want to investigate.

Before regularly attending gatherings at the mayor and Seamstress' complex, I felt left out of cultural happenings. The mayor's weekends give me tastes of trends. Reading magazines, for example, selling designs and body types to me, the customer, who the designers would have no interest in as an individual person. To be honest: reading those magazines made me feel left out, excluded. I'm looking at pictures of, reading articles about, people who would have no interest in me. Still, those magazines kept me in touch, before I had the actual contact through the complex created by the Seamstress and the mayor. Their guests include movie and rock stars, fashion editors, and the socialites who wear the designers' clothes. There are also "regular" people (the complex fees are on a sliding scale). I like this development of the mayor's estate, because it allows me to witness trends first hand, even spend some time with the trendsetters, and those who mix with them.

When I lived in the city I got ideas from walking down streets. Out here, considering my reluctance to go into the city, I've relied on magazines for my understanding personalities, which wasn't the most efficient, since by the time a trend appears in those pages it is so watered down. Articles about trends, and those who set them, are far from dead on accurate; establishing distance is crucial to their structure. There are the journalistic limitations, and the points of view of editors. But most important is the balance publications must reach: marketing trends and trendsetters to the mass audience, while also protecting trends and their setters from that audience. This is where pumping gas and fixing cars comes in. My direct line to a variety of personalities.

A large number of guests drive out in sports utility vehicles.

■

Last night I decided to speak with the Physh about Trowt, his clothes and the mayor. I told her what I loved about Trowt was what I loved about his clothes: practicality. She has seen his room, his clothes. She has seen the virtual rose bushes. She has tasted my cooking (so influenced by him). We both have connections with the Seamstress. I want to take her to the mayor's. I don't think she'd be interested in high-profile guests, or teachers (she seems so well

PUMPER

grounded). Maybe I will try to make the visit during the week, usually non-crowded.

How unusual that I, the investigator, always open up so much to Physh. But then I think I understood that that was how I invited Physh to open up to me. She went into the heartbreaking details of her family loss, saying she was now geared up to mend her heart and mind; the very desire that links her with DR. Neither expects a full recovery, but that doesn't stop their quest for healing.

■

It dawned on me gradually that the Seamstress and Trowt were siblings; but was solidified when she tells me a story about her brother who she had previously referred to as Selmon, as Trowt explaining how he got that nickname. Members of an experimental band he played in in college started to call him Trowt, and it stuck into his adult life, but she still called him his given name, Selmon. Her brother Selmon was my Trowt; the Trowt I knew. I was deeply drawn to the Seamstress—now I see there is a visual resemblance between her and her brother. She told me the simple facts of their history, which I'd also heard from Trowt: the mother died when they were both young children, the father who hired a childhood caretaker who took over maternal responsibilities quite well, and in fact wound up coupling with her father, but not until she and her brother left home. This brother Selmon and she were close. I noticed the past tense, which she used in a way that made me suspect they were estranged, not that he was dead. She talked about their childhood, their adolescence, but rarely about the adult, post-college, relationship. Just that he was a musician, chef, and distractingly beautiful.

But once I learned they were siblings, what was I to do with the information? I was in fragile territory. I had strong feelings for these siblings, which in my mind were quite separate, compartmentalized, in no way bound together. I felt loyal to both; having Trowt's sister so close by was potentially explosive. I decided to adopt the sit back and wait strategy.

This is a problem an information gatherer like myself can face. What responsibilities do you have with each piece of information you collect; what responsibilities accompany information gathering?

For this reason, recording information is a sensitive area for me. If I have sensitive information and do not record it, maybe it will be lost. But if someone finds it—if I die, or if my home and records get broken into—then I could harm someone by documenting it. If that person wants the information to be kept secret. But again if I don't record it I might forget.

Thinking about this disturbs me, but still doesn't start any perspiration.

SEAMSTRESS

*W*hy design; why my brand of it?

Fashion treads a fascinating terrain: that space intersecting ways individuals dream of operating in the world, and the ways they in fact operate there. Fashion—like any profession—incorporates visionaries able to sustain fertile careers, with those who flash on the scene promisingly, then go on to serve up goods under, or over, cooked. Some are damaged by acquiring too much too quickly; others run out of ideas. Failure also comes from not paying careful attention to personal limitations, and strengths.

A booming economy, or some other form of financial support, can make a designer bold. Such expression might take the form of cleverly ornate, richly eccentric attire; yet sometimes simplicity is the boldest way to go. Unadorned is risky;

it can be glamorous, or monotonous. The pure suit, the uncomplicated slip dress, requires a sound knowledge of basics, together with a creative flair. Otherwise the piece risks dull and drabness.

My potency as a designer stems from interest with variations on the following questions: What does an individual *hope* to radiate from appearance; what does the person actually radiate, and what separates (if things do, and things often do) those two points. I'm not implying this is deliberately reflected in my clothes, accessories, dishes and beds for humans and pets, only explaining the questions which fuel my productions.

Appearance always radiates something, but what?

Take this question, analyst-like, to the couch. Use it to examine individuals' choices of shoes, hair, accessories, clothing and skin treatments—I mean tattoos, facial hair, body pierces, make up—and you'll learn a tremendous amount concerning someone's hopes, fears, dreams, troubles.

I've been enriched by psycho-analytic sessions with their focus on dreams, emotional patterns, speech, yet always wondered whether information could be gleaned through analysis of my appearance, which I personally put considerable thought, expression, even philosophy, into. In fact, one of our weekend guests was telling us about a new, flourishing analyst training program titled Appearance Analysis; the program trains participants to carefully assess clients' presentation: belts, hair cut and color, even choice of car or cell phone. In long term cases, analysis extends into the home:

what fills a medicine cabinet, choice of living room furniture, bedroom sheets, window treatments.

All this attention might make a customer self conscious. An analyst examining their socks or eyebrows; looking inside their garage or den. I think it would be hard to dress for such a session, and maybe you'd want to redecorate. But then the speech required for the talking cure kinds of treatment makes many people self conscious too.

Appearance analysis might work effectively for someone like me, fairly verbal, extremely visual, and capable of expressing myself through clothes, accessories, interior design. I believe my watch and belt choice express as much about me as any sentence. I do not believe this is the case with everyone's watch or belt choice. The mayor, for example, puts little thought into his choice of personal style. Unless dressing for an event or a party. But for someone like me personal style is expressive. Still, this approach (appearance analysis) may not contain the methodology to include ethics, which the verbal psychoanalysis—from what I understand—claims to.

Appearance radiates something but what? Brains, wealth, insecurity. Sexuality—passion for, disinterest in, that mind/body function. Food and drug addictions. Loyalty to traditions, desire to twist, even subvert them. This can be subtly apparent in outfits, or can be expressed in what comes close to costumes. Consider the suits—from power to cat—which express different kinds of authority (executive, dominatrix, stock broker, politician). Or more theatrical references to kinds of magic: scary (vampire, witches and warlocks), sweet (elves, fairies). Or out and out dramatic figures, heroes (divas and knights), or victims (maiden, fallguy).

And then there are political/spiritual choices, like everyone's individual feelings toward wearing leather and fur; or where the clothes were put together. I, like many in my industry, had a vague, nagging guilty conscious about this. It became chillingly coherent once the mayor asked me if I knew who made the carpet in my apartment, the gym shoes on my feet; did a human or machine construct them, did I know the age of those who made them, did I know how much the laborers were paid? He went on to say such products are often the result of slave labor. My assistant and I now pay careful attention to such human rights issues, whether we are purchasing something for our home or office, or constructing and manufacturing our own productions.

My brother Selmon's high school home economics teacher taught that appearing badly dressed was disrespectful to others. Selmon, Nantor and I disagreed. Cooking and sewing with Nantor taught us that dressing badly is not rude to others, it—like eating badly—is rude to oneself; both poor dressing and eating detract from the quality of an experience. We had friends, especially in high school, who engaged in bad manners and dress as a joke, or adolescent rebellion, which is different than engagement with either behavior as an adult unconsciously.

Just as you can buy expensive and inexpensive bad food, you can buy expensive and inexpensive ugly clothes. I will say that the most horrific clothes I've ever seen have *not* been budget. Pricey pants, blouses; three-piece-suits made from bad material and cut poorly break my heart. You find these everywhere. Far worse, the expensive pieces cut well out of poor material, or—the truly tragic case—a sloppy cut out of fine fabric.

I, personally, dress to feel creative. When dressed correctly, I generate my best work. Whether someone sees me in the outfit, or not.

Although, I'm never displeased if someone, say the mayor, drops by unexpectedly and pays me an appearance compliment.

Some—not me—believe black attracts negative energy.

I adore black; find it practical for walking the streets of any large, dirty city, as well as dusty country roads or muddy rural fields, but of course do not wear it all of the time. In the city we—my assistant, our design crew and I—wear black belted long coats over clothing determined by that day's specified dress code. We have monthly schedules. The code is different for each day of the week. For example, one week Monday may mean something plaid, Tuesday anything roomy, in any color, Wednesday something white. I might wear my white tank shirt dress, someone else a jumpsuit, the assistant might wear his big sleeved paper blouse over loose cotton drawstring pants and white loafers. That is when inside; outside he'll cover it all up in his black belted coat, and wear white shoe protection in the way of thick soled black over-boots. Obviously this is only when the weather is cool; in warm weather we lose the trench coat, and wear dark, open toed sandals (these mornings, employees wash their feet—likely soiled after commuting to work in our dirty city—as soon as they get to work; each has stacks of moist and dry towels piled at his and her individual work station). Thursday might be a denim, leather mix. Friday, a pant. This is just one example of one week. Code changes from one week to the next.

It continues to fascinate me, what an individual wants from a look, say, teetery—sometimes but *not always* painful—high heels, the backless dress, heavy, difficult to remove make-up. Or the edgier look, midriffs, low slung capris, or brainy: glasses with heavy rims, full cut skirts or pants under boxy tops. And there is the baggy vs. tight fit debate. No doubt baggy is more comfortable, but can it be attractive? I believe it can be, especially if you consider that wearing tight clothing for short periods may look, and make someone feel, attractive, but wearing them for long hours can produce psychological tension, body odors, even bacterial and yeast infections. I've seen that happen. Though that decreases if the material is made of natural fiber.

My most creative line started a few years back as a direct tribute to Rhulera, who continues in my life as a full force presence. It was based on the apron. Multiple kinds of people wore them: those people who loved cooking, those people who never cooked but had no strong feelings regarding that discipline, those people who despised it and used the apron as an ironic comment on the practice. Despite that success, I went back to my own design style, producing outfits more wearable than intriguing.

SEAMSTRESS

I love a challenge. Unchallenged, I feel puffy, short, disruptive, and I don't necessarily mean physically. My favorite challenge is the something special that can spark when two people work well together.

The mayor and I spark because we complement one another. He operates fully in the present, I long term plan. He is verbally articulate. I'm mildly verbally articulate; visual composition, on the other hand, has always come easily.

When I first met the mayor, he was a rising film star. I saw him at a reception, bottle of mineral water cupped in his fingers, looking incredibly beautiful, relaying funny, vivid stories; mimicking characters.

I was at the party because: the costume designer who worked on the latest movie the mayor acted in (a deconstructive western) had used some of my apron line for the actors.

When we sat down to talk, what the mayor told me he most liked about the entertainment industry, were the people. Not all the people, he emphasized, but some of the people. He talked enthusiastically about some of the people; some survive, others are devastated by getting too much too quickly: money, fame, houses, clothes, fans. He rambled about his love for organizing, about being elected class president consecutive years in junior high school, high school and college (even elementary school, too). He also talked animatedly about another hobby: investing. He successfully played the stock market, which brought him financial and personal freedom. People, investing, leadership, people; these were his favored topics. Where, I asked, do entertainment, acting, stand up comedy fit in?

Performance, he said, looking identical to Euge's father and Rhulera's husband, is a blend of commerce and art. He got so many jobs in the entertainment industry because he was well liked; people enjoyed him, wanted him around. He has a gift for mimicry, for faithful reconstructions; faithfully reconstructing he calls it. Not only with people's behavior and speech, but also for details, and order, of events. As a result, he didn't find his entertainment jobs demanding. I felt he was taking his talents for granted, and told him so.

He agreed, but elaborated. Explaining that performance is not his destiny, organizing is. Creating, and managing, a structure where people can explore independence, community, hobbies, spirituality, food, personal grooming. He believes the cruelest people are steeped in a sense of victimhood, of feeling powerless. Boredom, also, can bring out terrible behavior in people; people behaving horribly as a way to try and break out of numbness. He then went on to describe his lifelong dream of developing a complex where adults could relax, study, eat, exercise, recreate. Our conversation went deep into the night, and this is how our collaboration on the country community got started.

■

My designs became successful, I hired a brilliant assistant, my dog died, I started to take weekends for meditation and spiritual healing. The first time I went on a meditation sit after I met the mayor (I'd been going on these weekend sits a few years by this time), and my teacher started with the phrase, Meditate about a friend, someone you care deeply about, but not someone you feel sexually attracted to, I realized my feelings toward the mayor. And I had to keep them in check, not because he looked like Euge's father, Rhulera's husband, but because I believe it is wrong to desire someone who does not desire you. But then, sensing the mayor return my feelings, I let myself go ahead and desire him. I'd had relationships since Euge, but none which impacted me like the mayor. Many of those post-Euge relationships, as I said, tossed and turned in bed. There were other obstacles. I did not want more children; many younger men want those. And with older men I'm always worrying about their health, even those with good eating and exercise habits, because most of them spent years indulging in bad ones.

But the mayor, he is something else.

Maybe, if reconstructing events for memory is my goal, I should comprehensively detail incidents, even if I do not want to. No doubt I've bowed to my urge to rush through certain events, understanding I might—at another point—want to come back and dwell there. My goal is some sort of faithful reconstruction. I can faithfully reconstruct clothing (name an era and style) but am not sure about events. In fact, I'm writing this document to practice remembering; when I think of the past, things start to blur, I can't separate them individually. I hope this recording helps me to separate past events individually.

SIMPLY SEPARATE PEOPLE

Then again, maybe writing can make you forget.

I don't think of myself as a secretive person, though I didn't tell my family about my babies. My family learned all about Rhulera's death, Euge and I falling out of love, so understood why I decided to leave the university's rural region for the bustling city my brother lived in. Anyway, dad and Nantor's one year long spiritual journey turned into a much longer one. We got a letters, just after the twins were born, explaining that they learned/decided they were physically attracted to one another enough to live as husband and wife. But those letters stopped and we have not heard from or seen them since their departure.

But before that, before the birth of the twins, and the spiritual departure, when we visited my brother in college, and met members of his experimental band, is the time I consider special for us as a family. We all were heading new places; and my brother got a new name; we heard his band-mates call him "Trowt." Selmon explained his bandmates started calling him this during practice, and it stuck, adding we could call him Trowt instead of Selmon if we want, but he wouldn't insist.

I never told my brother about the babies, because he was caught up in a career change. Having suffered temporary debilitating illness from oat allergies, he switched from music to cooking and was studying hard to be a chef.

I've been overprotective of Selmon/Trowt; he has always been so beautiful. These are stories, reasons, but not *the* reasons I didn't tell my family about the babies. So I wind up a secretive person. No one, not even my assistant or the mayor, let alone my family, knows about my children.

Trowt and I were always close; we had small spats but no great arguments. Until he found out about the twins. I'd seen my brother fragile, I'd seen him sweat, I'd seen him sad, I had seen him sweet. I had never seen him in a rage. And when he learned about my children, who I concealed from him and my whole family, he went into a rage, his form of it anyway, which—I learned—was stony silence. Maybe I got so interested in the mayor as a way of blocking out the upsetting interaction between me and my only sibling.

In any case, I wanted to heal the stark bleak relations between my brother and me; we needed a healing eruption, but I put it off as I do with so many meaningful incidents.

■

When my skin began to change (sag, pouch, line) I felt it didn't express me. I felt strongly that my largest organ misrepresented me.

I know, from working so long in fashion, how beauty can disrupt. I've encountered many people with extraordinary beauty, and I know it can be distracting; the beauty can effect what it is the beauty is trying to say. What is trying to be said is distorted by the extraordinary beauty. I've never been a beauty, but I felt my aging features diverted attention. That someone would look at a recent forehead wrinkle or neck sag or eye pouch. Instead of listening to my ideas for a design. In reality, I think the process diverted only my attention. Nevertheless, I conceived of a fashionable face cover made with weather-dependent materials—light, heavy, waterproof—as a way of achieving the effect you get with hair brushed forward, long bangs, glasses, painted lips, scarves and turtle necks: face covering. But once I got used to aging, my looks and communication merged again, and my face covering interest turned into a design that made tremendous profits; I made a Glacial-Face-Wrap for times individuals must spend extended periods outside: shoveling snow, long, chilly chair lift rides at ski resorts, fitness walking; jogging, or gardening, in sweltering weather. A scientist friend of mine saw the design, and added her twist: a patented system of copper coils which regulated air flow and temperature and kept outdoor workers and recreaters warm or cool, depending on the temperature.

■

Work with the mayor and his complex tightly connects to my desired levels of personal growth and challenge.

I'm considering selling my own business, or passing it on, to my intensely creative and hardworking assistant who is young and driven enough to stay out late, smoke, drink, and still be on time and productive the next day. He has a brilliant knack for keeping up with, indeed just ahead of, trends. I tend to let myself get stuck in the past, or at least the familiar.

The mayor wants to create an environment people can be a part of. Earlier, I made the point that bad dressing shows a disrespect for others. Well, the mayor and I believe it's the

SEAMSTRESS

same with our complex: we wouldn't have inattentive meals, decoration or activities. And would not encourage bad table manners.

The mayor likes the idea of people focusing on activities. That focus prevents people from not liking one another, just because of opinions. The mayor believes judging one another—positively or negatively—because of their opinions can be a way of distancing, or superficially connecting.

Stating opinions isn't interesting, discussing them is, says the mayor.

So when he was elected to take charge of this small, rural town with increasing traffic from heterogeneous bustling cities, he wanted to weave these principles into all plans he set for the community.

What appeals to me about the challenge of the mayor's complex, among other things, is the diversity of participants' tastes. For example, the doughnut and wine reception I offered one batch of guests last weekend. Donuts and wine is a food/drink combination that turns the stomach of plenty of people, me included, yet it drew a huge crowd of those who enjoyed themselves. The wine was cool and full bodied; the doughnuts were crisp outside, moist in (we made them with the requisite wet, sticky dough), but the combination seemed naughty. And the people who came got along so well.

■

I'm not disagreeing with those who say if you spend a life of work focus, you end up lonely. But families, or other kinds of intense relationship focus, require deeply personal obligations. Not breezy social ones, but deeply personal. I know myself well enough to know I am not good at those. I prefer the action packed day. The minute to minute activities that require thinking and motion but not authentic love.

And I adore being alone.

Love comes and goes. Business does too, but it extracts a different set of demands.

■

Who would have guessed that my older brother would turn out to be so conservative, or at least concerned with family values? When he found out about my children, he actually tracked them down, and spent months with them, Euge and Bry. He wrote me epic letters, describing the twins, who, I learned, were very loving—especially close with one another—active and happy. Among their hobbies: horse back riding, cooking, acting in plays. Both, now in high school, were excellent students. He describes the first meal he cooked for them: grilled chicken, dandelion greens with lemon and garlic, fig stuffed cookies, iced tea. He describes how he hopes dad and Nantor are still alive somewhere, and will meet these grandchildren, adding how hard it has been on us not knowing their fate. Did they turn so spiritual they spun out of our kind of existence, or did something unspeakable happen?

I read the letter to the clickety clack sound of beaded curtains, colorful piles of new samples stacked expensively beside me, thinking this information at once saddens me, and validates my decision to have left them with their father and Bry. Had I stayed, they might be walking wrecks; I certainly would have turned into one.

At this point in my life, I find myself thinking of dad, Nantor, Rhulera, but don't let myself relish memories too much. I believe that relishing memories too much is a sign you don't look at the present, or toward your future. Relishing memories too much can become a romance with the past, and a sign you hide from responsibilities of the future. I get this feeling with designers who design products which have a hand made, arty look. Anyway, Trowt has written that he is coming here with the kids, Euge and Bry.

I know they will love the complex out here, will easily get along with the mayor and the Pumper. But how will I behave toward them, and them toward me?

BRY

*I*f I die prematurely, I want our children to have my version of events, so I am documenting. Understanding this documentation expresses my personal slant on things.

We called her the Seamstress, because she sewed all the time. When our relationship started, I was in a position of authority; as it progressed, she assumed one. She moved out here for college, and I was assigned to be her Big Sister; show her class locations, restaurants and bookstores; guide her through any problems feeling lonely, or homesick. But then, in an unconnected decision, she was assigned as my math tutor (I've always been weak in that subject). Authority shifted again when she got pregnant; I helped out with information and errands. She sewed during our tutoring sessions.

In my first college psychology class, we learned one theory

about handwork (knitting, stitching, sewing, embroidery): that type of activity was a substitute for self-stimulation, the masturbatory kind. The theory stems, I believe, out of intense spite, and inadequacy. The Seamstress, like other sewers I know, had multiple abilities. Math for example, a design flair and teaching skills. Her patience, indeed compassion, for my math situation, allowed that aptitude—never strong, but not as frail as I'd believed—to surface. Patience, compassion, then, were additional Seamstress assets, and you'd have to add serious inner and outer beauty.

I never believed in handwork's connection to self-stimulation; that the Seamstress sewed while I worked math problems was not what made our sessions erotic. Learning situations in themselves can be highly stimulating.

My math lessons started about the same time the Seamstress and Euge began doing everything together. Some class mates even made comments about it, how out of state female students attract the best of our local boys. But that wasn't fair because out of state male students went out with regional girls just as often. What surprised us was less how much time the Seamstress spent with Euge, than how much time she spent with his mother, Rhulera. Rhulera, immensely successful in her kitchenware business, was a benevolent, distant presence in our town. Highly respected, polite to her considerable number of colleagues, business contacts and family friends, but especially close to no one; everyone found it odd to see her so often with someone the way she was with the Seamstress.

I had known Euge since elementary school. Known and

liked. Looking back, things are distorted, but one true thing: I wanted him for my boyfriend, or at least for my math tutor, and felt displaced by the Seamstress. Even before she got pregnant and got the affection of his mother, even before she started occupying everything Euge-related.

But now, a decade and a half later, I see things differently; I am grateful for the Seamstress; who knows if she didn't somehow contribute to the beauty of the life Euge and I share now. For whatever reason—true love, good chemistry, mated souls—we are that rare, happy couple who talk, horseback ride, walk; take our yearly vacations with the kids, and romantic ones without them. We have frictions—being a Stepmom is not always easy for me. But I was able to focus on founding the pre-school I've always dreamed of; an institution which grew wildly successful, some say even started a national trend, and helped put our small, rural college town on the map. Though it did not bring me the degree of personal satisfaction I had hoped.

Now—to our huge surprise—Euge and I learn I am pregnant with twins.

My parents were teachers; I started off that way: went to Educational School, taught first grade. But my focus, my fascination, was always early childhood development (explaining my desire and ability to help the pregnant, and then, later, mother to newborns, Seamstress).

Back to the school. While our community had good teachers, what we needed was a day care/pre-school to help out all our working parents when their children were young, pre, full-school-day. The economy was changing; our rural community could no longer support itself through farming. Mothers and fathers started to work in the businesses and factories sprouting up all around our area, and/or getting degrees at the college. We needed high quality care for our babies and young children; a special place for them to play, learn, be supported. The success of this school came from a combination of cooperation with the college, good planning, community support, and of course, luck.

Our methodology for child rearing and caring does not include systems leading to isolated child/adult interaction, but ones that create more extended family, group settings; this is one cornerstone of the school's philosophy. Obviously, a child must be and feel loved, have a safe structure to operate in, be stimulated. Also, we believe children need to move. Physical activity is key, and we have complex climbing equipment in and outdoors. Food is important, our kitchen is checked regularly by the health inspector. We work closely with the local elementary schools (when I grew up there was one, now there are three) to ease students' transition into them.

We believe that healthy child development includes children watching adults, not just interacting with them. Adults, in our view, are responsible for making colorful, interesting lives for themselves. This sets a good example for children.

I started as the Director and have continued, though I might take some time off after giving birth. Have I mentioned I'm newly pregnant, and with twins?

SIMPLY SEPARATE PEOPLE

I, and others, have explained the school fully—analytically, anecdotally—in other places. It fell into place easily, logically; maybe for those reasons I don't feel it was such a challenge. My professional arena is one thing, my focus here, in this document, is personal. Not, I know, that you can so easily separate the two.

It was possible for me to work full time, even with the twins, because of my father in law, Jorje, who takes an active role in our family childcare. Euge and I would have put the twins in my pre-school, and only did not because Jorje, an excellent caregiver, and colorful personality, expected to take care of them. And we don't argue with Jorje, when he steers things in a certain direction.

I believe in paying attention to trends in your life, and in making changes accordingly; a view Euge has helped me cultivate.

I'm trying to be truthful here, because the truth can be interesting; sometimes it is lies that are dull. But I can't harness truth, really, I'm still working through my perception of it, and of course how I want to be portrayed. I can't really get out of that. Wanting to give a favorable impression of my intentions, appearance and character; a positive self-spin.

Some teachers and counselors stock up a storehouse of aggression. A hockey player or cutthroat businessman or rock and roll performer can express aggression—in fact their professions depend on expressing aggression—in public. But teachers and counselors—mothers and fathers for that matter—have to deal with their aggression much more covertly.

BRY

Mine builds up; I'm not always able to keep it in check. What sewing did for the Seamstress my school hasn't done for me. Gardening, weeding and horseback riding are helpful, but it's this pregnancy that has really changed things. I sometimes worry that my unchecked energy prevents me from being the best wife and stepmother a woman could be. Sometimes everyone irritates me; I respond by leaving, heading outside to garden, or walk. But when I mention this to Jorje he smiles and says that it's better when kids are used to some degree of reality—for example the fact they can be annoying—at an early age.

I rarely get annoyed at school, where things are blindingly busy.

I would like to say here how I love the Seamstress despite the affection she got from my husband's mother, and the fact she—not I—had the family's biologically produced offspring (this current pregnancy is so recent). I do love the Seamstress, and did sincerely help her during her pregnancy, even when it looked as if she and Euge would be long term together. Still, the bug of envy bites me about these other issues. Rhulera, who never gave me more than a passing glance, loved the Seamstress. As a daughter, colleague and friend. The Seamstress, same age as me Seamstress, had been special to Rhulera in a way I never was, never would have been even if she hadn't died. I understand why the Seamstress left; she wasn't meant to live in our town with Euge and the kids. I admire, even envy, her life. To be that rich, powerful and independent.

SIMPLY SEPARATE PEOPLE

While the twins did not have a biological mother or grandmother, they had a loving stepmother in me, a loving father in Euge and, as I mentioned their devoted grandfather, Jorje. They learned a lot about stories from their grandfather. But truly, they popped out special, which I can assert without any kind of bragging since they are biologically unconnected to me. And I don't just assert their specialness at birth to sound generous, compensating, in other words, for some aggression surge.

Although that sort of behavior would fit into my personality.

The first years Euge and I were together, we carefully used birth control; we had his twins to take care of, and the idea he was incredibly fertile since he insisted he "pulled out" every time he copulated with the Seamstress. The twins, he maintained, were a result of pull out. But after a few years we thought we'd like to expand our family, stopped the birth control, and "tried" to get pregnant. It didn't work. We went to traditional and holistic specialists; no one found any evidence of infertility. So after awhile we just accepted our family size and never thought again about birth control.

Then.

A decade and a half later, shortly after Euge returned from his annual Horse Whispering convention, I started feeling all those pregnant signs my colleagues and friends had made me so familiar with: mental and physical weakness, food repulsion and cravings, tender body parts. I went to the Doctor. Sure enough I was pregnant, and with twins.

Don't you ever father anything *but*, I asked Euge, feeling a surge of reassurance, ok, rapture. Things between the Seamstress and me now seemed to be evening up. And, strange enough, my due date was around the time of the twins' birthday.

The pregnancy was surprising, but not as surprising as the timing of what happened next: I learned I was pregnant just at the time Trowt came to town, introduced himself as our twins' biological Uncle, and stated his desire to take them—with us too if we wanted—to meet their mother.

The problem with documenting is figuring out the order to explain events and people who figure in the documentation. Euge for example, I have a hard time describing him, because we are so close; I can't find the distance I'd need to depict him. Anything I write that is Euge related seems inaccurate. Distance, geographic or even death, I think, helps you describe a loved one. Because it gives you some perspective.

Let me say something about an important figure I've mentioned but not flushed out and do have perspective on: Euge's father, Jorje.

Jorje believes in past lives, and believes that he had lived several, and was in the habit of dressing up like one of his past lives and telling that person's story. These visits to the past, or maybe I should describe them as a merging of past and present, change as quickly as every few days, months; some of the personas last years. Over the years I have seen: a thespian turned town mayor, a Doctor, a painter, the mother of a large family, one of the first families to trail blaze their way and settle out west (he believed he came back in different genders).

When the Seamstress was here, Jorje lived as the famous thespian-turned-town-mayor. After that it was the pioneer mother whose husband nearly broke her heart (I learned my cooking here), a persona which lasted several years after that, at least until the twins were just out of diapers. Next came the painter. His project as a painter was to record landscapes, and day to day life in our current town before it was populated. During this painter period, Jorje worked tirelessly in the study he converted into a studio. I remember him moving around his antique table stacked with watercolors in slippers, waving his hand, as if stirring air when he spoke. His works portrayed stimulating, extreme climates: summer dust and heat, winter ice and wind—weather which sometimes required you to stay indoors; in winter because of the bitter cold, in summer because of the blistering heat. Also portraits of simply beautiful weather, such as a lucid watercolor he titled "Billow" which hangs, framed, in our kitchen. Everyone agrees that you can truly sense the spring day he depicts; feel the warm wind, see the pale sun, moving clouds, smell the fresh grass. That's history. Those days there was nothing to see except creeks, trees, fields with variable surfaces. Now, in contrast, he says, our developed town ground is hard, smooth, predictable. And the view: condominiums, strip malls, cul de sacs.

Still, there is something in our town, something left of the raw, wild pioneer courage.

I love our town; I can easily do things I like, such as horseback ride, walk, grow my own fruits and flowers, make jam.

It's hard to say what Jorje looks like, because he changes periodically, but he always appears fit and attractive. Jorje visits his past lives in different ways. Sometimes he just lives them, other times he speaks them, sometimes he adds physical documentation. During the painter period I just described, he makes and keeps a special journal by sewing together brightly colored squares of cloth. This word/picture book functions as a fascinating historical record. For example, he documents one Christmas Eve when he was a young boy by painting a picture of a large, elaborately decorated tree, and writing this text below:

> A pulsating moon shines over miles and miles of snowy, unpeopled prairie. Mother wears, in this coldest of weather, a fringed shawl tied around her head and a wide leather belt with a bright buckle—one thinks of bull's horns—around her waist. She stands tall, erect. Father, a gentle, carefully dressed, odd man sits in a chair next to her, fingers wrinkled at the joints, veins standing out at the backs of his hands. On this Christmas night he's re-telling the story of his travels to this country, how weeks on a boat moving through the ocean made him famished for fruit, how he can never again eat salted fish. My brothers and I are sitting on the floor, wearing our red neck cloths and green pins, as we're asked to do every Christmas. I try to hide the fact my throat is sore, because I want to go on the sleigh ride, and then eat the cookies shaped into horses, roosters and stars and decorated with burnt sugar and small hard candy we helped mother bake yesterday.

SIMPLY SEPARATE PEOPLE

We all feel Jorje's visual/narrative constructions teach us about the past in a way that makes an impression.

I had not just been upset that I got the Seamstress, not Euge as a math tutor; I had always, from the time I was a little girl in elementary school, loved Euge. I know there was visible pain in my face the first time I saw the look he gave the Seamstress; it was at a party for math tutors and their challenged students. I felt deep shame afterwards, hoping that no one saw the feeling my facial expression had to reveal.

I know things happen for a reason, but I can't help but think my life would have gone better if I'd gotten pregnant younger. Maybe I wanted to feel even with the Seamstress. Maybe then my aggressions would not have built up. After getting pregnant, I lost that anxious, prickly feeling I often had; pregnancy satisfied something my successful school did not.

For starters, it dramatically improved my eating habits. But that might have had something to do with Trowt, who believed in food that was interesting to taste as well as nutritious.

When Trowt first came to visit, our town was impressed by the dashing figure he cut: tall, handsome, well fed and carefully dressed. Euge thought he looked like the Seamstress; he picked that up before I did, probably because the children resemble Trowt and his sister. I like to think—in fact what I sometimes feel the first years of my marriage were based upon—is that the Seamstress figures more prominently in my mind than in Euge's. Even when he looks into the faces of our children. Their children.

The twins resemble Rhulera too, Euge and Jorje less so. Though, as I indicated, given Jorje's persona alterations, it is difficult to define his features.

Trowt affected us in many ways, starting with food. Although my food tastes already were transformed by pregnancy. In fact, friends, Euge and other family were shocked at my new, interesting eating habits. Pregnant, I had oddly healthy cravings: green apples, potatoes, romaine lettuce and lean sirloin. I could have eaten the sirloin rare, even raw, but concerns over bacteria convinced me thorough cooking was essential. Pre-pregnant I had a bland, fatty diet; pale, dairy oriented foods; anything with cheese, cream, whole milk: French toast, pizzas and pastas drenched in white sauces and macaroni and omelets. I always leaned toward these foods, then learned to cook them during the time Jorje reenacted his life as the mother and cook for a Pioneer family and their many hired hands. He taught me recipes for puddings, breads, cookies, soups, roasts. And truly useful tips: Don't make hot cereal in flimsy pots; you'll scorch the cereal, possibly scratch the pan. Make only as much hot cereal as you can eat, because cold or re-heated cooked cereal is unpalatable. Heat dinner plates by wrapping them in a clean dishcloth and setting on a bench or coffee table by the fire or wood burning stove. (Trowt later taught me to place them on the upper rack of a dishwasher during its drying cycle.) Store potatoes with an apple to suppress sprout formations. Fill a teapot with warm water before steeping the tea. Always keep a bowl of ice water in the kitchen when you are working with heat and sugar.

The combination of my taste preferences and Jorje's hearty recipes contributed to my drift into that high fat diet, which had to be curbed. Pregnancy, Trowt or at least that combination helped to curb it.

You might wonder about my size, learning about the fatty food preference; I am the same size I was in college: not thin, not chubby. I do not exercise, formally, but live an active lifestyle without which I'd certainly be much heavier. Gardening, horseback riding, running a school and child rearing burn up a lot of energy. Without these activities I might have developed plumper, fleshier, face, fingers and body.

I don't know what Trowt thought our town's reaction would be to his visit. People accustomed to big, or at least heterogeneous, cosmopolitan, cities often dress and eat and behave in ways that seem strange to small, rural, homogeneous communities, even developing ones like ours. Though our college has always given us a hint of the larger world. Euge and I heard about Trowt when he came to town, before he visited us, from our friend, Kal, the restaurant owner, who told us about a customer who walked in, looked at the menu and asked if they could make him a mushroom omelet cooked in ghee. Kal asked what ghee was.

Clarified butter, the customer answered, pulling a container of something yellow out of his backpack. Ghee is sweet butter, clarified; cooked down until the water and milk solids are completely removed, leaving a rich butter flavor without butter's health hazards—ghee lubricates the joints, doesn't pool in them, which plain butter does, though ghee, like butter, is highly caloric.

And then went on to introduce himself as Trowt, a chef interested in our town because his sister went to college here.

He offered to show Kal and his staff how to make ghee, could he borrow a slab of butter? It was a slow time at the restaurant, after breakfast, before lunch, so Kal let Trowt in the kitchen. As Trowt reduced the butter he asked about the local restaurant business. After he made the ghee, Kal let him cook the omelet. Finally it was time to eat. Kal had to taste, and agreed the omelet tasted better with ghee. He offered to buy some, Trowt surprised him by saying, You've misunderstood, I'm not selling any; you can have mine, and anyway, I taught you how to make it.

This incident gives you some idea of how seriously Trowt takes his cooking and ingredients, and how convincingly he shares his fascination with others.

From him I learn that allspice, which I thought was a blend of clove, cinnamon and ginger was a pea sized berry from the evergreen pimiento tree grown in Jamaica. He teaches me how to effectively transport platters of food in the car trunk: line the trunk with pre-soaked beach towels to cushion the porcelain platters, keep them in place, avoiding any sliding around, breaking, spilling. He shares information regarding his recent interest in teas: how to pair with food, aspects of

SIMPLY SEPARATE PEOPLE

basic tea preparation, for example boil water for black teas, but not green. After one of our first family meals he served us all loose teas in vaguely familiar little teapots with strainers. When we asked him where he found so many individual pots he said, In the Rhulera section of the basement. Euge and Jorje were reminded of Rhulera's tea passion and teapot collection.

Trowt respected my food tastes, but much preferred his own, and convinced me to too. Although he sincerely appreciated my jams. But what I immediately loved about Trowt: although my type of cooking was not his favorite, he never treated my style with the blend of pity and spite you might expect from a world famous chef. He tolerated my creamy party dips, my method of corn buttering (thickly butter a slice of dinner bread, roll a hot ear of corn just out of the pot in it; this neatly coats the ear with warm butter, though it does slightly flavor the buttered bread slice), but never pretended to love or adopt my food tastes. He would politely scoop his first chip or carrot stick into a creamy dip, then eat the ones after that plain and unadorned. And he said he liked his corn unbuttered. He was generous with his opinions. After patiently witnessing me make my onion rings: huge and heavily battered, he said, Fine, as far as it goes. My choice of the onion group: leeks, especially for warm soups and salads. Leeks are very pretty, and they don't make you cry, even tear up.

He then proceeded to show me a delicious broiled leek recipe that he would serve instead of the heartier onion ring.

But he diplomatically went on to add, If you are leek resistant, just thickly slice a large Spanish or red onion, skewer all the way through and grill. Flip with tongs. You get the savory onion flavor without the baggage of the traditional onion ring's batter and oil.

And he suggested if I insist on using onion, I should slice it with the sharpest of knives, and near running water, to prevent tear flow.

Time with Trowt, and of course my pregnancy, have made me more open to color, protein and spicing. I can let myself get downright downhearted, looking back on the years of gardening I did, without appreciating the vegetables I've so dearly come to love. But things have changed; Trowt's salad never comes from a bag and now mine doesn't either, and I no longer make a salad drenched with mayonnaise, filled with chopped pieces of meat and cheese.

The twins call me mom, while understanding the facts of our (non) biological connection. When they were in junior high school we told them who their mother was—they always knew they had a mother who left them with their father, grandfather and me, they did not know she was a world famous designer. Once they learned her name, a well known name, they followed her life through stories about her in papers, magazines. They read about her dog's violent death from a speeding car; they knew about her talented assistant, about her recent project with the mayor: starting a complex out in the country.

Some cities sit forlorn, untended, vastly depopulated be-

SIMPLY SEPARATE PEOPLE

cause of residents and businesses fleeing to develop outlying suburban land. In contrast, the city the mayor and Seamstress come from is a frighteningly populated, densely cultured, cluster. The mayor and Seamstress' project (from what we read and watch on entertainment oriented TV shows, and have confirmed by Trowt) is an attempt to at once unclog their city's accumulation of money, businesses, people, and lessen social isolation of a lonely rural area by integrating some of the concentrated wealth and population of the neighboring urban environment into it.

We, all assuming, I think, we would meet the Seamstress some day, respected this plan. The twins expressed curiosity, but, surprising to Euge and me, and to my colleagues at the school, did not express such an urge to physically encounter her. Which I thought might be a defense mechanism; Euge understood it as a desire to protect him and me (their way of assuring us we were great parents); Jorje said it was proof they were advanced enough to comprehend the insignificance of biology based connections.

I'd say we lived as a happy family, and so did the peers we compared ourselves to.

When Trowt came to our town, though, on the heels of us all learning I was pregnant, we were prepared for a change. Our lives were headed for expansion, in a big way. Things were ending, and starting. Jorje switched personas, this time to his life as physician. And it was time for the kids to meet their mother.

■

BRY

We travel to the mayor's complex in our newly purchased recreational vehicle, with Euge behind the wheel. He is initially skeptical of this monster size mover, but loving to drive (wagons, horses, tractors, cars), he unsurprisingly takes to it instantly.

Despite bubbling, sometimes acidic, anticipation, we have a pleasant, even calm, trip. Our group chemistry is good. The twins, always able to entertain themselves, watch movies we insert into the RV's VCR, then reenact or rewrite scenes, line by line. I am very happy travelling so far with a bathroom, dishwasher, sheets, and no responsibilities except my bodily functions. Which at this stage of pregnancy are considerable. We stop every two hours so I can stretch, and walk. Trowt reads books and works on soups in the kitchen, which he carefully equips before we leave, and replenishes along the way. Jorje, re-visiting his life as a doctor, bones up on professional skills by reading holistic, popular, and academic medical journals.

We finally reach the complex, which surprises us visually, before we even enter, by its elaborate beauty. The mayor and Seamstress stand at the entrance, as if they've been waiting. We have kept in close cell phone touch during our trip; their presence is a welcoming sight.

The reunion is happy, emotional; we sob, hug, get embarrassed, then sob and hug more. Only Jorje remains steady. Trowt takes a few tender moments with his sister, then drives the RV to the gas station to get fueled and to visit the Pumper; the two, we are told, are deeply in love.

SIMPLY SEPARATE PEOPLE

He has some *explaining* to do to that woman, the Seamstress says in a way that makes us all laugh.

Within a few days we develop a routine. I rest and take short walks, the twins start a drama club, Euge stays by me and works in the stables. Dr. Jorje, who fascinates the Seamstress, I think, as much as her children, treats the mild illnesses and injuries that pop up here. And of course checks me regularly. We've had a lot of discussion over who should deliver the twins, and where the delivery should occur. Jorje's training is several centuries old, though he is modernizing, learning all about cleanliness, for example, and pain medications. But no one, least of all him, believes he should be our first choice of doctor to deliver the babies. Do we visit the local hospital the mayor says he can vouch for, or the city hospital he also vouches for, rated the best in the country, if not world. We consider natural, at home birth—there is a professional midwife out here—with Jorje and the local hospital as back-ups.

Jorje is concerned, and has convinced us to be, about hand washing in hospitals; saying that unclean hands are the most dangerous things in public health care settings. Unwashed hands can cause bloodstream infections that lead to devastating illnesses. Jorje takes the position that an at home birth allows the best opportunity to accurately monitor hand sanitation.

We are all enjoying our time here in the mayor's complex. The Seamstress walks around thanking her brother and looking awestruck at her children. She always was professionally ambitious. Maybe love has softened her. She and the mayor cut a desirable couple. Most of the time they are busy, overseeing complex activities, but we all see them looking into one another's eyes, holding hands, exchanging a quick kiss while bent over a set of architectural plans, sitting in the garden, watching the kids perform, eating Trowt's cooking.

Now that the Seamstress has achieved so much, I think she feels she can sit back and let herself enjoy. Once she suggested that the twins, who appointed themselves as being in charge of drama at the complex, with full mayor approval, could write and act in a play about the family's history and that she'd make the costumes. We all are curious about her fashion empire, and when we ask, she seems to down play her role, passing off credit to her assistant who, from the pictures I've seen, is stunningly beautiful. Yet we know from reading the papers, magazines and watching documentaries she, whether admitting it to us or not, built an empire.

I have been able to piece some Trowt facts together. He was a busy, highly respected chef in the city. The Pumper, with her then roommate/boyfriend had been his neighbor, before they moved out to the country. Trowt's interest in organic farming, need for periodic breaks from the city, and friendship with the Pumper and her then roommate/boyfriend brought him out to their place, now the gas station, in the country. The boyfriend moved, Trowt and the Pumper became romantically linked.

Trowt and his sister, the Seamstress, were always close. Yet the Seamstress, for her own reasons, which I respect, never told Trowt, or any of her family or friends, about the twins. When Trowt, in a round about way, found out about the children, he was shocked. He deals with his shock by visiting the spiritual teacher he periodically spends time with. After that visit he is convinced of his responsibility to unite his sister with her children, and their father, grandfather, even me, the stepmother. And grows determined to formally unite himself with the Pumper. Which he understands might be tricky since he disappeared from her life for that period; what must she have thought? But when he sees her he explains that he believed he must reunite his niece and nephew with their mother, that this reunion was linked to his reunion with the Pumper, and that the first must happen before the second.

Both reunions are successful. Trowt now lives with the Pumper, who we visit for gas, conversation and books. What the two share is clearly special.

We hear part of an unsettling story connected to Trowt's disappearance. He had made a batch of chocolate with ingredients that had harmful effects on consumers, more specifically on their pets. Apparently even the smell of the ingredients caused some pets to turn aggressive, even ferocious. People might have chalked this up to accident, but because Trowt disappeared just as this was happening, things seemed suspicious. There were journal articles, news programs, speculations in Internet chat rooms. Trowt, the Pumper says, cannot really re-enter his old life until he addresses the whole chocolate/pet situation.

But, I ask the Pumper, Has anyone asked him about it? Oh

yes, she answers, adding that she herself only learned his reasoning recently, when he returned. That she did not know any of it during his time away.

According to Trowt the pets went mad because of genetically engineered ingredients he unwittingly used in his chocolates. He is scrupulous about his ingredients, but something wrong got smuggled through in this case, and Trowt attributes it to faulty food industry policies regarding quality control. What happened was this: the human consumers who ate the chocolate were fine. But somehow the smell of the masticated chocolates affected nearby animals; it caused consumers' pets to behave strange and violently.

Trowt's response is two fold: First he launches a consumer education campaign to make shoppers aware of dangerous food processing procedures. Second, he has lawyers working to sue the government for poor food handling—growing, modifying, spraying, injecting, waxing, packaging, storing, distributing and supplying. He cannot legally discuss the case details. But Trowt believes that things we have done to our foods will harm living things in oddball, unpredictable ways. A pet behaving violently because of an odor, which was what happened with his chocolates, is in line with his predictions.

I agree with him, continues the Pumper, Though play the devil's advocate. I try to suggest that genetic engineering is a biotechnology that could address troubles sprouting from global population growth and the accompanying land diminishment. It could solve problems caused by crop loss, disease, infestation. Trowt vehemently disagrees. He believes the philosophy that goes with that type of *"revolutionary biology"* is the very kind of thinking that got us into trouble with our environment in the first place. And I have to say, Trowt knows his food science; he has researched gene engineering like he has every inch of my palm—Trowt loves peoples' palms, mine especially. He can and will tell you way more than I could but not until after the legal process is a little further along.

One baby, or both babies, flip, and/or kick; I yelp, tell the Pumper what happened, we smile.

I am mildly familiar with this issue of gene alteration and food crops because we dealt, or are trying to deal, with it in our town. Maybe because of Trowt's education campaign, farms in our area are starting to question the efficacy of spraying, modifying, versus going organic. And local stores are starting to question where to buy food; should they support local farmers, and if so, only local organic ones? My assistant at the school, who knows much more about this issue than I do, has recently and convincingly suggested our school serve children food and juices that are certified organic. Trowt's eyes glistened when we told him this over tea one late night, and he did tell us about his dedication to organically grown foods, but not his education campaign. And he never went overly on about it, as some do about their beliefs. I make a comment to the Pumper that Euge, Jorje, the kids and I should learn much more about food production and processing. She gives a short bark of a laugh and says if we spend more time with Trowt we certainly will.

Trowt and the Pumper live in a magnificent structure of hidden libraries and closets, built by Trowt and the Pumper's former boyfriend/roommate, who is now off travelling. She has somehow managed to plant and maintain rows of flourishing rose bushes, even off-season. They are virtual, she explains, when I visit a few days after our arrival, as she takes my hand and leads me around fascinating home and grounds, not perhaps as elaborate as what the mayor and Seamstress constructed, but just as engaging.

I wonder, but don't yet ask, what Trowt—with his faith in things grown organic—thinks of her virtual rose bushes. Instead I ask, Why the gas and auto repair? For a steady income, she replies. Then adds that it provides her with the people contact she needs.

Listen, she says, switching subjects, taking my hand, feeling my belly (she knows, because she asked, I like when people feel my belly; some pregnant women do not), I have a dear friend coming out to visit. Well, several friends actually. People recovering from intense grief.

I wonder, does she know about Rhulera. And she must know about Trowt and the Seamstress' parents, not yet returned, the Seamstress told Euge and me, from a spiritual journey they embarked on before the twins were even born?

Without answering either of these questions in my mind, she launches into a speech: We all cope with grief differently. Some lug the whole carcass around, huge and unpenetrated. Others poke into it bit by bit through memory, recalling, telling; others sublimate into art or another activity, or find consolation in spiritual union, believing the person's soul will travel to heaven, or be reincarnated; others may approach it with a sort of philosophical spin, voicing the koan, 'Who dies?' Some of us fall deeply, madly in love with our grief. Some retreat from life. Some fill up with increased purpose and energy. We all heal differently. The crucial healing (it may never be total, it often occurs bit by bit) can happen through environment: loving, stable, soothing, robust. I believe this complex provides such an environment; I know the mayor and Seamstress founded it in part for healing purposes. My friends coming to visit lost family; one lost her entire family, another still has a sister. I hope you can meet my friends when they visit. Not, she says rubbing my belly with a laugh—we both feel one or both babies' kick—that you'd need to address anything directly. Your presence, I mean you, your husband and father in law, the twins, all this coming together, it radiates something fine.

I understand her points. Healing can seep in from things around you. Facing it, or anything so fragile, aggressively, or even too head on, can be counter productive.

I've often thought how there can be a pureness, even dearness, to intense grief.

The Pumper continues, My friend, Physh, has tried overcoming grief by talking about her recovery period, even memorizing it to play, and replay again. Physh (she lost her entire family) and her partner DR (he still has a sister) heal themselves by talking, not about the tragic events that damaged them, but about periods in life they consider healing. Some health professionals call the moments post traumatic.

I ask her opinion about medication as a way of controlling emotional pain. She says she believes certain medications can help shrill pain; people who, maybe not even because of a tragedy but because of a biochemical configuration hear voices or see things, medicine can help these things. But as with all emotional unrest, support systems can help with everyday decision making: getting out of bed, making the bed, deciding what to wear, what to eat, where to go.

I agree with her. My school works with children who are for the most part too young to medicate, but I've seen our elementary schools medicate some of the children after they went through our program. Even our elementary schools understand that such medicine has to be used together with other supportive structures.

Now, she says, Tell me about you. Your parents, for starters, up to how you and Jorje met.

I'm happy to talk to the Pumper. But I want to document this strategy of hers: she gets people to talk, often by sharing, or seeming to share, some of her own information about herself and others. I explain, Grief, how we all deal with it. My mother, so helpful professionally—she was one of two women teachers in our entire district—suffered what people would now call mood swings. Some days she would go to work, but come home only to stare at the wall; slip away, helpless to tug herself back, oblivious to our attempts to. Other days she would go to work, then come home with the kind of energy that generates flurries of activity. Mother loved crafts: cutting, gluing, sewing things together. She was a large woman, very able with her hands, highly organized. She sewed or knit many of our clothes, and arranged all of them perfectly, season by season. Holiday items were also made by hand and labeled; this container for carving roasts, this one for baking utensils, used once or twice a year, this other one for seasonal decorations. She had no interest in cooking. That was my father, he baked everything from scratch: bread, noodles, yogurt, ice cream. I only knew about canned soup from my friends. My father was straight middle of the road: not desperate or happy, not handsome or ugly, not kind or cruel, not sharp or dull. His job was professional high school teacher, but he spent his free time cooking. I was never that close with my twin sisters, sixteen years older than me. While I did not grow up in a close family, I've gone on to build my own tight knit, if unconventional, one.

My parents did channel energy constructively, but it did not seem to bring them enjoyment. In contrast, Euge's parents both channeled their energy with a splash. Politics, painting, cooking, horses, sports, musical instruments. And his mother Rhulera was famous for her lucrative, and bustling, food and kitchenware businesses. I learned to channel energy into horses (riding, tending), and gardening, and as I mentioned when I got older by cooking pale, high fat foods—comfort foods one of my well-thumbed cookbooks calls them; foods which hold so little appeal to me now. And I was always interested in children.

While I wouldn't call my parental relationships close, they did no damage. When I was little, just before starting elementary school, I was very close to an uncle, my mother's younger brother. He traveled a lot and wrote me letters. Not to me and my sisters together, just to me. I still remember a line from one letter he wrote in an airplane and said, "And now I see a little angel, who looks a lot like you, flying in the sky." I loved this uncle. He made everyone really laugh. In fact, the hardest I ever saw my mother and father laugh was around this uncle. But he died of an illness when I just started school.

So, the Pumper says, Jorje might resemble something of this uncle for you.

She has a point. I didn't know whether to tell her anything about Jorje's visits to his past, or even if she knew anything about them.

I sometimes wish that Jorje, with all his abilities to time travel, would return as my dead uncle. But technically it is impossible since they would be the same age; I'm pretty certain Jorje only visits his past lives, not past lives in general.

I once wanted to get Jorje a collector's box, a cabinet or curio as they are called, to exhibit evidence from his various past lives. When I shared this idea with him he said, with a smile, You and your documentation determination.

Then went on to say, No thing dies; things only flicker in and out of view.

What Euge remembers as a child regarding his father's persona changes, and his relationship with his wife is fascinating, quite sweet, and could be the subject of an entire new document. Maybe I'll get to it.

SIMPLY SEPARATE PEOPLE

I decide not to discuss Jorje with the Pumper, but do tell her about Euge, my childhood crush on him, how I felt when he made love to the Seamstress. I tell her about the school, my relationship with the twins, which brought me up to how I feel about the present.

Nothing is missing from our life, yet coming up here to the complex—even though we've just stayed a few weeks—I feel I can express a different side of myself. For example, one thing being here does: frees me up to look. At home I work, eat, drive. I don't look. I don't ever just sit to look at, say, a person, sky or landscape. At home life is active; we labor, we move, we talk, we don't watch. Unless it is a school play or a movie or TV.

Being around the Seamstress one is, naturally, more attentive to looking, at least at clothes and ways people dress.

The Pumper has a nice, casual style. My own clothes are functional/shabby (the Seamstress kindly but untruthfully uses the term functional/chic). I've recently become desperately sick of my wardrobe, and not only the pregnant clothes, which are huge, but also the normal clothes I packed for after the birth. The Seamstress, familiar with my pre-pregnant weight, which hasn't changed since college, though things have shifted around here and there, made me some clothes for wearing after the baby, assuring me she made them intentionally roomy.

She tells me, You'll need some clothes in-between your pregnant and normal size; your normal size doesn't always come back so quickly.

Some pieces are designed specifically for nursing (which I plan to do). These clothes she makes for me are simply wonderful: fashionable, practical; easy to wash, sturdy fabrics. Will I bring these clothes home? YES! Our local college draws a national, even international, population, but not people who dress the way the Seamstress does. There are shops out here near the complex, like the world famous sweater store. Fashion reigns in this rural community. Though I don't feel out of place in my own clothes, and don't think my husband and children do either. Anyway, I look forward to giving birth, being a new mother, and wearing new clothes.

The Pumper smiles and tells me that the Seamstress has given her the best clothing advice, and in the most sincere and helpful way.

■

After much discussion, and some premature contractions, we decide to deliver the twins in the highly rated hospital in the city. The mayor and Seamstress know an excellent ob-gyn there. And the hospital staff convinces Jorje each one of them is a scrupulous hand sanitizer. In the city we meet Physh and DR, the Pumper's friends, and see the Seamstress' magnificent home and business. In the beginning, Jorje, Euge the kids and I stay there with the mayor and Seamstress and her crew. Trowt and the Pumper stay out in the country, keeping an eye on things at the complex.

While the twins are fascinated by the complex, its activities, its different regions, the guests flooding into, and out of, it, they are more blown away by what they see at their mother's business in the large, thriving, very dirty city. When we reach the city we park our RV, impossible at least impractical to navigate through busy urban streets, in a lot, and drive DR's sister's sports utility vehicle. The Pumper's friends Physh and DR are living just across the street. When we first meet them I worry I'll act awkwardly, knowing what I know of their sad pasts. But neither puts out any deep sense of pain, only concern about me and my condition.

The Seamstress' business runs like a well-oiled machine. Her small, beautiful assistant—he is more beautiful in person than any of the pictures or TV footage I ever saw of him—and assertive staff dress in fascinating clothes they somehow seem to coordinate with one another. (When I ask about this the assistant explains to me that their dress code includes a broad range of daily themes: plaid, denim; vintage, futuristic; relaxed, close fitting.) These attractive people come and go, sip things out of paper cups, eat lunch with chopsticks, speak multiple languages. Travel. And the neighborhood that the Seamstress lives/works in is filled with stores selling interesting soups, shoes, jewelry, meats and breads. The twins are smitten, so are Euge and I but Jorje tells us, What you find in the city are those who need to draw attention to themselves. Riveting entertainment is fine as it goes, but easy access to entertainment can make you lazy in what you see. Do you still see the beauty of the mother spooning baby food into her hungry toddler's mouth while strolling in the park, or supermarket?

See, these people who live in this cosmopolitan city have the kind of success and good looks that are acceptable to our culture. Look how magazines, TV, even books document their achievements, lifestyles, ideas. What interests me, personally, are all those single, separate persons leaning, loafing, feeding, earning. Cooking, singing, transporting, bathing.

Then Jorje veers into new terrain:

I know what it is to be unnoticed. I know what it is to be neglected. I once loved someone who was unfaithful; when I was the mother of that Pioneer family, my husband was in love with our beautiful widowed neighbor.

Sometimes when Jorje talks I don't know how connected his opinion is to him now, or to his persona of the period.

He continues, You know what consoled me? The fact that I had much nicer skin than the woman my husband loved; in that life I took care of my skin. In any weather, windy falls, icy cold winters, blisteringly hot summers I paid attention to moisture: water to drink; cream to nourish skin. And another thing I learned, so as not to become devastated by my husband's love for another: I worked to make anyone, everyone fall in love with me. And it worked. I learned to channel deep affections toward my children, our community, our homestead. Even though my sons were grown and always at school, or home working or riding, they were strong and I was proud. I grew quite attached to our house, its furnace, plates and sheets, all totems of consolation, all things which provide pleasure, and a structure that generates effective behavior on my part: good cooking, parenting, charity work. No one wrote poems or plays about my life, and that was a

SIMPLY SEPARATE PEOPLE

heroic life. By far the most heroic one I ever lived, and the life that brought me the least amount of attention. That experience taught me that the real heroes, the real fascinating people, aren't these showy ones you see here in this bursting with wealth and culture metropolis. These city people interest but don't fascinate me. They occupy enough peoples' attention. And I am not saying wrongly so. But they don't need to occupy mine.

I feel for the life Jorje lived, but don't agree with him. True, some people here draw attention to themselves. But I see, and the Pumper, who I've talked to about this, agrees with me, a lot of people happy to be engaged and to be anonymous. I think Jorje forgets how much attention people can draw to themselves in a small town. Think of when Trowt visited, for example. But like I said, this might be more connected to Jorje's present persona as a physician.

When my contractions begin, we actually walk to the hospital, just a few blocks from the Seamstress. Though the births take a long time, in the end everything goes fine. For the next day or so, I think of nothing but the births, I run the event through my mind again and again. Now I cannot remember anything except the surge I felt when those two came out. Surge of what? Of pain and pleasure on a physical level; of fear and rapture on an emotional one. It has been said before, I cannot say it better. And I remember after the birth, Jorje walking around passing out candies, crooning: Sweets, sweets, sweets.

The mayor and Seamstress come to visit in the hospital.

Since travelling out here, I had seen the Seamstress frequently, but had not spent time alone with her. She visits me just as the R.N. lists tips on nursing the twins. After the R.N. leaves we spend some time remembering the Seamstress' nursing experience, including Rhulera and my attempts to help her. The Seamstress talks about Rhulera, saying she never makes a business decision without wondering what Rhulera would have done. I always knew the Seamstress loved Rhulera, this moment helps me understand the depth of that devotion. Her face appears sad, yet soft and she soon changes the subject to Jorje.

She talks about him, starting off telling me that when she met the mayor he reminded her, almost eerily, of who Jorje was when she lived out there. Now she wonders, did he re-enact some past life, while also enacting someone else's—the mayor's—present one?

Jorje then so much like the mayor, now.

I find myself telling the Seamstress things about Euge and me, and Jorje.

These are the things I don't mind *talking* to someone about, but am reluctant to *write*. Secrets seem more perilous in the form of written documentation than speech. Words *can* be recorded, but they usually aren't. They usually disappear into air, or a version in someone's memory. Written words on the other hand are visible solid, tangible.

Jorje's personas, as I've said, are pretty above board; doctor, watercolorist, thespian turned politician, pioneer woman. Except one period I start to describe to the Seamstress; a period which only lasts a week (very short amount of time for Jorje), and starts not long before Trowt comes to town. Jorje's appearance turns sort of wolfish, and, embarrassing to me, deadly sexy. Everything seems deadly sexy: his walk, his jeans (they turn tighter fitting, lower riding), his penetrating eyes, his white teeth that seemed to grow wider and longer. He holds his same erect, handsome figure, but seems deep in thought, though not morose, and his complexion changes: it grows blotchy, the way a teenager's might. His day time activities slow down, lucky for me the twins are in school all day, old enough so I no longer rely on him for child care.

I tell this to the Seamstress who pales, reaches toward me, and says, You are serious aren't you. I nod. She continues, Does he uncharacteristically sleep most of the day, does he go through this period when Euge is at a Horse Whispering Convention (which he visited twice every year).

Yes, and yes. She continues. During that "wolf" period, does Jorje pace a lot at night, do you encounter him at night, standing familiar yet not, holding out his arms. It's Jorje but not Jorje. Does some magnetism draw you into his arms, pull you to lead him by the hand to your bedroom, to mount and be mounted by him, and when he leaves you do not see him, as if he had disappeared.

More yes's.

Our encounters with him were identical, except hers was years earlier, on the grounds of college campus dormitories. Mine was on our own farm grounds, nine months ago.

And then she whispers, Don't worry, Euge didn't father the older twins either. He thinks he did.

The Seamstress and I start laughing uncontrollably.

See, I couldn't even be honest in this documentation; I never hinted the story behind my pregnancy. Somehow now, though, it isn't such a secret so I can document my babies' lineage more honestly.

PHYSH

*D*R's sister calls to tell us she will be gone two more seasons. Her business related travels are doing that well. She tells me that she has just met a small group of photographers who invited her to their next shoot, a camel fight. The sport is apparently quite popular in parts of the world she has been visiting. They tell her they find remarkable how camel owners become deeply attached to the camels they train. This makes her miss her own pet; she asks about the dog, with more feeling than usual. After I give her details—food intake, exercise amount and type, sleep, general mood—she thanks me profusely for taking such careful care of her pet. I tell DR's sister I've grown to deeply love her dog, and all of the activities caring for her requires: walking her, sleeping with her, grooming; I've even learned to give her a bath. I started this when her personal dog groomer was unexpectedly called out of town, and now look forward to it as an enjoyable part of our daily and weekly schedule. The once a day brush and de-knotting, the warm suds of the weekly bath, the drying off, the mopping up the very wet bathroom floor. DR's sister, voice, broken with emotion, thanks me, adding she is too moved at this point to discuss any businessy details; she'll call back tomorrow and we'll cover her messages, mail, errands she needs me to run for her, and so on. She says she is excited to stay away two more seasons, but that she so misses home: her brother, her neighbors, her pet. She asks me to tell her brother she loves and misses him, and thanks me for taking good care of the two most precious living things to her: her sibling, her canine. She says if DR wants he can reach her on her cell phone, otherwise she'll call back tomorrow; by then she'll have a hotel room at a mountain ski lodge where she and several clients will spend the week (unless she decides, last minute, to join the photographers on their camel battle shoot). I tell her I know I speak for DR when I say we both miss her, and look forward to her return, but surely understand her need to stay away two more seasons.

Directly after this telephone call, DR comes home with the dog and a box of powder cookies. We eat one, and feed the dog her special biscuit, as I give him the newest news on his sister. He smiles, suggests she might be in love, adding happily, I would even say proudly, that she has found her way to recover, to move on from, to not get swallowed up in, their personal loss. He adds that she has always been the one in their family who was best able to love from a geographic distance; that her love is loyal, deep, even fierce, but absolutely best expressed at a geographic distance.

We eat the cookies from a plate we set on the ottoman she made for me, which has not come unraveled since my slight but necessary repair, despite the fact we use it as a bench, foot stool and even table. DR then says something I find surprising, pleasantly surprising, he says that he and I, like his sister, have navigated our way admirably through our bleak period of family loss. I realize he is making a point: things have changed, we are busy with new duties and people.

DR and I met, and started this recording of events as a kind of restoration documentation, in a recovery group for individuals who have suffered personal loss. The group, which was time limited and run by an student intern at the hospital just near DR's sister's apartment, started off with the leader encouraging participants to speak of whatever they wanted. Some detailed the loss and ways it made them feel, others focused on memories. DR later described these sessions as authentic, helpful, indispensably sad. I agree. Just before our last meeting, our grief counselor, headed out of state for graduate school, made a suggestion which brought DR and me together: Choose something you associate with healing, with continuing your life, dwell on that something, draw out, detail. There may be different versions of the story, she tells us, we should feel free, then, to tell and re-tell. A new session would start up with a new student intern. DR and I declined to join the new session with the new student intern, but started narrating, memorizing, versions of our own healing periods. This document records a portion of mine. It is I talking to DR about a period in my life after losing family. DR documents his own experience in private. He reads his document to me any time he or I want, but prefers to do his recording alone and in private. I cannot channel my energy in that way. DR can spend time with his recovery period and pen and paper or laptop and word program and record. I cannot, I get too distracted, my energy jumps here, there, here; I cannot confine it. But talking to DR keeps me calm. I talk, DR records; this process shifts my mind from the blankness I felt for so long. The effects seem to be solid and long lasting, though who can know for sure.

DR remarks that his sister heals best while off functioning in her flurry of activity; she carries pain with her, yet she is not stopped by the pain the way he and I sometimes seem to be.

Of course, we both say at once, things have gotten very busy.

The Seamstress stays out in the country, but her house here is full of visitors, including a woman bulging with her soon to be delivered twins. Her name is Bry, and she is not only close to the Seamstress but to the Pumper too. DR and I are not yet entirely sure how. Bry, her husband Euge, their teenage twins move into the palatial Seamstress' quarters. How did this come about? This family needs to be near the hospital just a few blocks from the Seamstress' home and business so Bry can deliver the twins there (this neighborhood hospital is rated number one in our city, perhaps even the country, some say the world).

And the family grandfather, named Jorje, turns out to be not only a physician but also a master tailor, and ready to shift from the one career to the other. He spends a lot of time with the assistant; the two converse constantly about their new line of clothing. The Seamstress, according to both the Pumper and Bry, is completely wrapped up in the community she started with the mayor, and more than happy to relinquish her business and design duties to two fine talents: her assistant and Jorje.

Trowt has come back into the Pumper's life and she radiates with happiness (and relief that she kept enough faith to not alter his wardrobe, or doubt his integrity). She explains the chocolate mystery to me, which she herself only recently learns. Trowt believes that genetically engineered ingredients he unwittingly used in the chocolates the animal owners ate generated the violent behavior of previously pacific pets. She is thrilled to learn I have some unopened bars, locked up, thanks to DR, in a vault. She says Trowt will need them as important evidence in the lawsuit against the food industry he is embarking on.

More than the family moves into the Seamstress' home/business; a puppy moves in too. The illustrator develops an allergy to dogs, so asks the animal loving assistant to adopt his puppy. After checking it out with the Seamstress, and learning that DR and I will happily include the puppy in our frequent dog walks (DR's sister's dog has strong maternal instincts and immediately accepts the puppy into her life), he agrees.

By the time the twins are born, DR and I spend good chunks of time with this puppy and the assorted people living and/or working across the street. It seems surprising yet sensible that these disparate strands (Pumper, Seamstress, assistant, dogs, neighbors), weave tightly together. I still visit the Pumper when I can. I'm back to working a few afternoons a week at the music store, while also maintaining my disciplines of learning, practicing, exercising and documenting with DR. With his help I complete all his sister requires of me. We also help Bry with her newborn twins, which she has come to rely on DR and me for, or maybe she just expresses this to us, knowing how soothing it can be to feel depended on.

[LYNN CRAWFORD]

lives outside of Detroit with her husband and two children. She is the author of Solow, *a collection of fiction, and* Blow, *a novella.* Simply Separate People *is her first novel.*

Black Square Editions
[EDITED BY JOHN YAU]

The Footprints of One Who Has Not Stepped Forth
[RICHARD ANDERS]

The Garrett Caples Reader
[GARRETT CAPLES]

Simply Separate People
[LYNN CRAWFORD]

Painting
[JEAN FRÉMON]

Extracts from the Life of a Beetle
The Recitation of Forgetting
[FRANCK ANDRÉ JAMME]

Fathom
[ANDREW JORON]

me With Animal Towering
[ALBERT MOBILIO]

Bayart
[PASCALLE MONNIER]

Ecstasy Shield
[CHRISTOPHER NEALON]

Echo Regime
[JOHN OLSON]